THE WEBBING BLADE

THE FIRST CRYSTAL KINGDOM NOVEL

RAYMOND S FLEX

1

ON THE RAMPARTS

THE CLOAK BILLOWED out in the wind behind Ma'reygar. He felt the stiff, cool breeze blowing in from the north. A slight scent of roast pork carried on the breeze, making his mouth water a little. His staff dangled from his hand but he kept his grip tight about it. He felt his calloused fingers find the deeply embedded ruts there. Those ruts he'd worn in there. In the middle distance he heard the babble of laughter drifting upwards. If only they knew he was here, they wouldn't think to laugh. They'd grab for the hilts of their swords without a second's delay.

He stood up on the battlements of Ilsnare Palace. It had been easy to get inside, to get into. A few mind hexes and the odd paralysing curse and he'd got right up here. And now he was inside there was nothing they could do to stop him. He was too far away for the Council to do anything to stop him even. Before they caught an idea of what had gone on, what he'd done, he would be far away and the curse would be impossible to overturn.

He stared along the ramparts, picking out the pair of guards dawdling about up there, talking among themselves. They both wore swords at their hips, and a crossbow dangling off their shoulders. In the flicker of light from the burning torches hanging off the sides of the ramparts, he could make out the faint lines of expression on their faces. Their crooked smiles, their matted eyes and the few worry lines in their foreheads. Neither of them saw him, neither of them even so much as glanced in his direction.

It was almost too easy.

Ma'reygar kept to the shadows. He brushed his gloved hand along the stone wall as he approached them, mumbling the hex beneath his breath. This hex would keep him hidden till a counter hex was uttered. They would never even see him. All they might register would be a slight waver of the clean air about them, and then it would be too late for them too.

He stood only a matter of steps from the two guards now. The two of them continued to chatter away between themselves, making some joke about their boss, a man called Herimyre, Captain of the Royal Guards. They might joke but if Herimyre had been there he would've sensed there was a mage in their midst. He might have had a chance of saving the two of them.

But he wasn't there.

And so Ma'reygar could cast the killing curse without a moment's hesitation.

One of the men dropped dead. Stone-cold dead, grasping his throat. His skin turned pale and his eyes lolled back in their sockets. All that marked his fall was a tiny groan which escaped his slightly parted lips and then the slump of meat wrapped in cloth as he dropped onto the stone of the rampart.

Ma'reygar turned his attention to the other guard.

The other one was on his knees, doubled over. His shoulders rose and fall with the exertion of his breathing, as the fire crackled away in his chest, burning him from the inside.

Ma'reygar approached him, crouched down, and reached for the man. He seized hold of his hair in his fist and yanked his head back so that he could look into his face. "Where's the king?" Ma'reygar said, his voice gruff through his gritted teeth.

The guard stared at him with wide eyes. His lips trembled as he tried to speak. And then Ma'reygar saw that the guard's hand, shivering almost uncontrollably, was making its way down to his belt, to the hilt of his sword. The loyalty of some of these guards was beyond belief.

The differing resistance to magic, though, was to be expected.

Ma'reygar supposed this guard had some magical blood in his line, somewhere a long way back. A shame that no one had noticed it, never thought to teach him to fully understand it. He might have been able to fight back. But the very fact that he had the blood in his veins was just enough for him to resist these few of his dying seconds.

Ma'reygar could make it easy for him. Mutter the killing curse a second time. Better for him to end this here right now, to put the man out of his misery. Summon a fresh torrent of flames to burn within the man.

But, no, he would cause the man to suffer. Just a little. He deserved it. He was as guilty as the rest.

He was allied with those that had taken *her* from him.

Ma'reygar reached for his own belt and unclasped the buckle keeping his dagger in place. He slipped it out of its sheath with the lightest scraping of the blade against the leather holder. He breathed in deep, savouring that rich, earthy scent. He could almost taste that dank earth in his mouth. He could almost certainly hear that snickering sound of giant spider fangs scraping, one against the other.

He felt the freezing cold of the blade in his hand, passing right through its well-bandaged handle. He had had to wrap as much cloth about it as he could, to keep the chill from freezing his hand right off. And still he wore gloves whenever he handled it. The blade always seemed to get colder whenever it sensed death nearby, or the prospect of a life which it was soon to end.

Ma'reygar watched the guard's hand shudder on its way to the sword hilt, before growing uncontrollable. Yes, the fire was truly taking its hold on the man now. In a matter of minutes the man would be dead.

But Ma'reygar hadn't time to waste.

And if he left the man alive, to live out his final shuddering moments of life, there was no telling what he might do. He might raise the alarm. He might bring Herimyre to bear on all this, and Herimyre was the only one who could possibly stop him now.

In a single, swift movement which betrayed the appearance of his old bones, Ma'reygar lurched forward and grabbed hold of the guard, spinning him round so he held him tight around the chest, and so that the blade tickled the man's throat.

He watched its dull grey, razor-sharp edge sink into the surface of the man's skin, a smear of blood appear on the blade. "Tell me where the king is," Ma'reygar said, his voice steady and cool.

He felt the man shuddering in his hold, his whole body seeming to enter some kind of a frenzy. Then, through his chattering teeth, the man got out, "In his chamber . . . he's in his chamber." And then, with a strength that belied his induced fever, he craned his neck round, his whole head shaking uncontrollably, and met Ma'reygar eye. "That . . . that blade, what is it? I've never felt anything so cold."

Ma'reygar kept his hand impossibly still, the blade still at the man's throat. And he continued to look him right in the eye now sure that he saw some magical blood in there somewhere, still fighting hard against the curse.

Against the flames.

It was a pity the man had to die. If someone had unearthed him, told him of his potential, then he never would've joined the Royal Guards, never would've got himself on the wrong side of Ma'reygar's grudge.

But that was all so much speculation now.

As Ma'reygar stuck the blade into the supple skin, slipping it in behind the man's windpipe, he said, in a gentle, almost fatherly voice, "This dagger. It's called the Webbing Blade."

He withdrew the blade from the man's neck, and let the guard fall away from him, into a heap alongside the other one.

Dead.

He wiped the Webbing Blade carefully with the hem of his cloak and then headed on along the ramparts, to the king's chamber, to finally get his justice.

2

BRINGING IN THE YIELD

LOUSON DORF BROUGHT his scythe soaring, making it whistle as it displaced the air, and felt the slight, satisfying tremor as the blade caught the stalk and sliced it in two. He watched the stalk as it fell and then landed at his feet with a slight rustle.

Right on top of all the other stalks there.

The sun beat down on him from above, baking him out here. He felt the sweat dampening his hair beneath his straw hat and he reached up to wipe the thin layer away with his index finger. He could smell the dust rising all around him as the other labourers worked the fields, chopping down the corn, 'bringing in the yield' as they referred to it around here.

He could stare right to the horizon, to where the fields slanted downwards with the curvature of the land, and he could still make out the labourers, not much more than blurry dots, all of them in constant motion, with their own scythes, slicing away, just bringing in the yield as busy as he was.

Today was Midsummer's Day and the last concerted effort to bring the yield in, to ship it off to market so they could all get some money to put bread in their own mouths.

Their crops went all the way to the capital, to Ilsnare, where it would feed all the rich folks that lived there, all the rich folks that charged them taxes, those taxes that got Capital Road built and Hnet Eaemur's little daughter Calli sent along it to a medicine woman. And then later it'd paid for her to get patched up by the medicine woman.

There was no doubt in Lou's mind that what they did was good, honest work, and they got their recompense for it rightly. And although they might not have the finest things, and although some days it seemed like their budget might not stretch to an extra flask of ginger ale, he supposed himself to be happy.

Or near enough to it not to care all that much.

But he had no reason to think about such deep matters as happiness, really, he had to get his portion of corn in before the sunset. If he failed to do it by then they'd have to turn in. There was no option these days. The cursed animals. Their ragged undead corpses would spring up from wherever they hid from the sun during the day, and they would come hunting.

Anyone caught out in the fields after dark would be killed.

Or left for dead.

Lou held his hand up to shade his eyes from the beating sun, and judged, by the position of the sun in the sky, that it was getting on for about half four in the afternoon. He had another hour or so to bring his yield in. Old Man Junth knew how it was for the working hands, the lean winter and all. He was a fair boss. And so he paid out a winter's supplement.

But if Lou's yield came in under weight then he'd be the one that'd get it docked from his wages. And, despite everything else, he just couldn't afford to lose out on so much as a grung. There was a hard winter just around the corner, rolling in, like there always was, and he had to stock up.

Work would be hard to come by in the coming months what with all the yield brought in, and no planting to be done till the next spring. There were other jobs, protection, serving as a skuller: going out of house during the night to beat back the cursed animals, to prevent them overrunning the village, but he'd never been all that good at that fighting stuff. He never could handle a crossbow, let alone a bow. And he was even worse with a sword. And he just couldn't so much as get started with anything bigger: a mace or an axe, his tender, slightly doughy muscles just wouldn't allow it.

Doughy, and he was barely out of his teens. No, one thing was for certain, he was a farmer. That was what he'd been born to be and that was what he'd be till the day he died. All he needed was a farm of his own, then he'd be able to support his family, then there wouldn't be any need to worry. *He'd* be the one doing all the hiring and the paying of wages. *He'd* be the one who got to dock wages from his workers if they brought in a light yield.

Lou whipped off his straw hat, wiped his sweat into his hair, smelling the biting saltiness of it, and then fanned himself with his hat just a few seconds before replacing it on his head.

He rolled his sleeves up to above the joint of his elbow and really got to reaping. He swung the scythe hard through the air.

Thwack. Thwack. Thwack.

Over and over again. His muscles drew tighter. His sweat made the handle slippery. And he tasted the corn dust hanging in the air, like a rough mist. When he looked around him he saw the hundreds of others, all of them swinging away just like him.

Bringing in the yield.

Before too long, the sun dipped down on the horizon, the very bottom of it touching the very furthest trees. Lou lost himself in that peachy glow just a little while, and then he crouched down, gathered up his stalks in his arms, holding them tight to his chest, before joining the rest of the farmers on their way to the weighing tent where, just like every year, Old Man Junth would plonk their yield on his big set of scales.

Just like everyone else, Lou eyed the horizon, watching the sun gradually dip downwards. In a matter of an hour or so the animals would be here, to ravage the land. And by the time they came they would need to be gone.

Long gone.

He peered over the ragged figures, working hands just like him, all of them stooped men with battered straw hats shoved down upon their heads. Their trouser legs were tattered and torn, covered in the sallow corn dust. Their shirts were untucked and soaked in sweat. The stench of body odour was overwhelming. Lou caught a whiff of just about everything in that crowd. That was the smell that he always thought of as a hard day's work well done.

He looked back over his shoulder to the field. Well, this year they truly had brought in the yield. The whole field was flattened, reduced to roots and churned up earth. It looked like the whole field had been stampeded by a herd of cattle. But it had just been men. Men like him. Their tread wasn't all that light after all.

One by one they shuffled forward in the queue, entering the darkened interior of the tent.

Lou looked over the tarpaulin, saw that it had once been blue and white stripes but had long ago faded in the sun. He wondered if one of Old Man Junth's sons had got it second-hand off some merchant from Ilsnare—it looked just like something the King of Ilsnare himself might spread out for one of those famous festivals of his, the ones that Lou heard about.

He could only imagine the songs in the air, the pluck of strings, the shrill notes of the flutes and the beating of the cattle hide drums. And then the food. Sometimes he would lie awake just thinking of it, his mouth watering and his nostrils flaring with those imaginings of his.

The crackling of a hog over an open fire, an apple stuffed in its mouth, its skin bronzed and flaked. The seasoned potatoes, and the mounds of tarts with their trickling honey icing.

It was enough to turn his stomach inside out.

As he shuffled further forward in the queue, he heard the neighing of the horses on the other side of the tent. Those horses would pull the carts along the country lanes, take them back to their towns as fast as they could.

He caught sight of a broad-chested man wearing a close-fitting black tunic open in a v-neck at his throat, exposing his wiry charcoal-coloured hair. He carried a sword down at his waist and a crossbow strung over his shoulder, both weapons ready to be produced at a moment's notice.

A skuller.

These were the men who roamed the lands at night taking care of the cursed animals, making sure that the rural folk didn't get mauled in their beds. These men kept them safe. But still, something about them sent a shiver round the collar of Lou's tunic.

Or maybe it was just the light summer evening breeze catching his perspiring skin.

Lou stood at the tent flap now, and he could make out the murky inside of the tent. There wasn't all that much in it. By squinting he could just about make out the cobbled-together wooden table, and the current working hand in there right now, his back to Lou.

Lou tried to get a glimpse past him, to the scale, trying to mentally compare his yield with the man's own. They looked pretty similar. Probably half a pound difference here or there, but pretty much the same.

And then, as he heard the muttered word, and the chink of a purse of grung being given over to the working hand, Lou caught a glimpse of the man at the table. The man who would be in charge of weighing Lou's yield, deciding whether or not he'd brought in enough to be granted his full payment.

Just liked he'd feared. It wasn't Old Man Junth at all.

It was his son, Herbert.

3

WEIGHING IN

LOU'S TROUBLES with Herbert Junth had started all the way back at the beginning of the growing season. Like all the men in his village, he'd caught the horse-drawn cart, hours before dawn, and gone out to work Old Man Junth's fields. He had been working Old Man Junth's fields for several years now, ever since he'd got done with school, or too bored with it, he couldn't remember which it was now.

This year, though, things had been different.

Lou had noticed the change right away. They'd barrelled along the rutted lane. He remembered staring off the back of the cart at the dust rising off the path, and hearing the rocks bouncing off the underside. He also remembered being pressed up against the side of the cart by a fellow working hand beside him.

He had smelled the man's oniony breath from his morning broth, and that mingled with the sour milky taste still in his mouth, all Lou had managed that morning as he'd rushed out of the sleeping house where his ma and pa, and little sis, Syre, hadn't even noticed him leaving.

His ma worked in the village as a medicine woman, selling her herbs about the village. She had been the one who had first told Hnet Eaemur that there was nothing she could do for his daughter, and why he'd had to leave the village to go out and seek help.

His pa worked about town as a carpenter. He helped people fix up their houses: fit new rafters, patch up leaking roofs, and sometimes, when someone had had a bumper year, help them build a house for their children to move into. He didn't get paid enough. Not enough for Lou not to have to supplement the household income as much as he could.

One thing that made Old Man Junth a good prospect was that he paid fair. No, better than fair, he paid *well*. And the winter's supplement was beyond a blessing. Old Man Junth had been a working hand too, when he'd started out, and so Lou guessed he still knew just what it was like.

Which was much less than could be said for his son, Herbert.

Lou's little sis, Syre was much cleverer than he was. She had a big pile of books and everyday she crossed a bunch of fields to get to a nearby village where there was a wise woman, a woman that'd once worked in the renowned Ilsnare University. Syre used words that Lou just couldn't understand sometimes. He always had to tell her to slow down.

Anyway, when the cart had pulled up onto Old Man Junth's estate, Lou had felt funny.

Just funny.

An odd feeling he'd just never got before. Never coming to

work for Old Man Junth. The only way he could think to describe it was that he knew that *something* was different. Everything seemed so quiet, almost deathly.

And then when he'd looked over to the path ahead he'd seen him. Herbert Junth, standing there waiting for them. He had his hands on his hips and a grimace spread all across his face. He wore nice clothes—clothes his daddy had clearly bought him. And once the cart came to a stop Herbert had barked at them, like a master would bark at his dogs, and what was worse was that all of them, every last one of the working hands, had jumped to it, bounced right down off that cart, eager to obey.

All except for Lou who'd skulked back, sat on the edge of the cart just a second, trying to position that odd feeling he was having, before going off to join all the rest. But that small act of defiance hadn't escaped Herbert Junth.

He'd spotted it right off.

And Lou recalled him uncoiling that whip from his belt, and then letting it loose so that it lay on the ground like a snake waiting to bite.

Lou had stared at it there, wondering just what it was for. And then he'd found out.

Herbert Junth had snatched his hand back, brought that whip up into the air with almost impossible speed, and then slashed the thing through the air.

Lou could still feel his cheek aching from where it struck him. The mark had bled for an hour or more, but he'd kept his hand pressed to it while he worked, not wanting to get whipped again.

Pretty soon he heard off other working hands that Old Man Junth had got ill over the winter and that he was pretty much bedridden—dying, some said. The upshot of thing was that the farm had passed into the hands of Herbert Junth, his eldest son.

And it soon became plain that Herbert didn't think much to the benevolent hand his daddy had used to run his farm.

He believed in fear. Cold and hard.

Lou held his hand to his cheek, feeling the welt there, the scarred skin. Although the pain had long since faded, the memory was still there. The rusty taste of blood in his mouth was still there. The smell of blood still there. That smart lash of the whip still there. And those piggy eyes of Herbert Junth's were still there, almost brandished into the back of his skull.

Herbert Junth dismissed the previous working hand and called the next forward.

It took Lou just a second to realise that it was him. That he was the next in line.

He shuffled forward into the tent. The whole place smelled stale, sun-baked tarpaulin, and he saw, over behind the table, the stacks of corn there, the pair of working hands putting it into piles, sorting it through, getting it ready to send off to the capital, Ilsnare.

Herbert Junth sat at the table jotting in a ledger with a quill. There was the huge set of scales beside him, the brass weights on the other side for ballast, to be measured against. And then, with a final flourish of the quill, Herbert looked up from the ledger.

Lou felt a cold wave pass over him. It was like that sensation he got after working in the sun all day, what he liked to call 'being sun-baked,' only this time he knew it had nothing at all to do with the sun.

He shifted up to the table.

If Herbert recognised Lou then he hid it well. He just gestured to the scales, for Lou to place his yield down there so it could be measured. Lou allowed the load to fall from his arms and onto the scale. He listened to the slight snicks and catches of the mechanism of the scales. He held his breath, but stopped short of puffing out his cheeks. He didn't want to show how desperate he really was. How much he needed this winter's supplement.

Herbert Junth squinted at the balance, those piggy eyes of his pinging from one of the scales to the next. Slowly the scales found their balance, with the yield outweighing the brass weights.

Lou had a sudden pang in his chest. Thinking about it, Lou had most likely outweighed the working hand before. He had done more than his fair share. And then, with a tickling sensation at the back of his throat, he realised that he wouldn't have to deal with Herbert till next springtime once he got his wages.

This would be the end for a year.

Although he had managed to avoid further whippings himself, his fellow working hands just hadn't been so lucky. Some of them had lash marks all across their backs, some across their chests, others had their legs covered in lacerations, growing into a crusty line of chaffed skin. Lou couldn't wait to go about the winter, helping out his pa.

It would be a kind of paradise compared with what he'd had to go through this year with Herbert Junth.

Herbert narrowed his eyes further, glancing between the yield and the weights on the other side. What was taking him so long?

Herbert called out to one of the working hands behind him, and the working hand came across to collect Lou's yield.

Lou watched on with just a smudge of pride as the worker placed his yield down upon the others. That would go to the capital, and it would feed people. His work meant something. Then he turned his attention back to Herbert.

Herbert reached across for his ledger, then reached for the quill. He dipped the quill in the pot of midnight-blue ink a couple of times and then wrote something inside the book.

Lou stood there, staring at his yield over there on the pile, and waiting for his wages, and his winter's supplement.

Herbert finished writing then dipped his hand into his drawer, fishing out a purse tinkling with grung. The cloth of the bag had once been a light brown colour, but was now so faded that it had a slight green tinge to it.

Herbert undid the string around the neck of the bag and tipped out the contents onto his ledger. With all the grung sitting in front of him, he slid off half of them to one side, cupping them into his hand, and then he dropped them back into the drawer. He replaced the remaining grung in the bag and then held it out in Lou's direction without a word.

Lou felt numb. His hands lost all feeling. It felt like his heart had turned to stone. The whole tent seemed to take on an eerie chill, and then, within himself, he felt a rage begin to pile up.

When Lou didn't take the purse, Herbert glanced up at him, then smirked. "You're not going to take your wages, then?"

Lou glared at him.

Herbert's smirk shrunk back on his lips and he scowled. "Is there a *problem* here?"

"What about my winter's supplement?"

Herbert shook his head.

"My yield was complete, I *saw* the scales."

Herbert's scowl progressed into a snarl. "Yes, yes it was. Perfectly complete. And for that you're to be congratulated. However, your dissent earlier in the season must be taken into account." He closed one eye as if calculating the side of Lou's face. "My rule is that if I can still see the scar then the lesson's still to be learned."

"I've done everything," Lou said. "Everything perfectly. I . . . I just don't understand it. How can you be . . . be so *cruel*?"

Lou regretted that word just as soon as he'd said it. Although he'd had the good fortune not to run across too many truly evil-willed people in his life, the few times he had done he had learned that it never helped matters to insult them.

Herbert barked out some order or other.

Lou didn't even hear it.

And, with a resolute swiftness, the skuller who'd previously been outside tending to the carts, arrived in the tent. He drew his sword and held it down by his side. He stood ready and waiting, ready to keep Lou in order.

Lou stared at the blade, the glint of the edge there, and he knew he would be no match for it. He turned back to the table, examined the paltry pouch there, his wages. He stooped over and snatched it up, then stuffed it into the pocket of his trousers. As he made his way out of the tent flap, back out into the looming evening sky, he heard Herbert call out after him.

"And if you show up for work next season I'll have you hung, drawn and quartered by way of example to the other working hands."

Lou felt that rage in his stomach twist and grow, the heat of it get almost too much to bear. And the worst part was that he knew he could do nothing. Absolutely nothing.

All was lost.

Next season he would have to find another farmer willing to take him on. But next season seemed impossibly far away for the time being. The biggest struggle would be even getting through the coming winter.

Without his winter's supplement his family would starve.

4

SEVERAL GRUNG SHORT

THE RIDE BACK to his village, Endmere, was a long and solitary one. All around Lou the other working hands buzzed with conversation, with their winter plans, with what they wished to do with their winter supplements. He could smell brandy wine thick in the air, taste the tang of it at the back of his throat every time he breathed in. He just bowed his head into his chest, scratching his forehead against the rough cloth of his tunic, and he listened to his heart beating, tried to lose himself to its steady rhythm.

He thought back to previous years. Through all the years when he'd come home on the cart, like this, he'd been so happy, delighted that his labouring was done till springtime. But the best part of it, *always* the best part of it, was the knowledge that tucked deep in his trouser pocket was his winter's supplement. The money that would get his family through. Allow them to survive another year.

Now, though, everything was under threat.

As he listened to the cart wheels clunk and skip over the rutted road, kicking up pebbles and hurling them against the wood, he did and redid the calculations in his head, somehow trying to make things work. But every time he got through with one calculation he came up with the same answer. His family would be doomed around the fourteenth month of the year.

In Giddlemarch they would starve.

A solid three months before he could get any work on a farm.

The working hands left off the cart as they passed through the villages, and he forced himself to be cheery as he bid them goodbye, and agreed that they'd meet up the following year. Lou didn't think to tell them that he would never be allowed to return to Old Man Junth's farm.

Not as long as Herbert Junth was in charge, in any case.

He thought back to that skuller, the man there with that enormous sword of his, and that crossbow, seemingly primed to draw out and pierce a man's heart in the beat of a crow's wing. If he'd so much as taken a step forward, looked to threaten Herbert, the skuller would've taken him down. Of that he was sure.

He thought back to the man's cold, pallid complexion. That was the same for all skullers, being that they were men of the night, they worked in the night. And the moonlight wasn't renown for giving men a tan. For other creatures, perhaps, but as far as man was concerned, they needed the warmth and light of the sun to live. And so, Lou supposed that was what had always bothered him about them. There was simply something intrinsically unnatural about them.

The cart jerked about as it rounded the familiar bends which led to Endmere.

Lou felt his body swaying with the motion. That knot of rage was still fixed in his stomach, and although it wasn't glowing as much as it had been back in the tent, when he'd been confronted by Herbert and that skuller, it was still there. And that was enough. Never in his life had he felt so completely powerless. Impotent. That was what he was. His family was going to starve to death this winter and he could do nothing to save them.

Only a couple of other working hands remained in the cart. They were both men from his village. Endmere was the last village on the route for this cart. The two men were best friends, and always had been. Their names were Eirk and Poels. They lived in neighbouring houses in the village and were always seen out and about together. Their wives too, Lou knew, were best friends.

They were a few years older than him, in their late-forties, perhaps approaching their last yield, and they always returned from the winter with hearty bellies full with ale fat, which they'd lose, as they had now, by the end of the summer. They would go back home to drink away their winter supplements. Their sons and daughters were already working, providing for their families. It might even have been possible for the two of them not to bother working at all.

And that sparked an idea for Lou.

He slipped the two of them a sidelong glance. They had their arms wrapped around one another's shoulders and they were belting out a lewd song, one which Lou always heard down the village ale house on full-moon nights.

An emptied bottle of brandy wine lay upturned between the two of them, rolling about the cart with each turn in the road. Both had their eyes shut and could've been anywhere else.

Lou wished that he could've shared just a tiny part of their joy.

It was Poels that noticed Lou looking and he instantly broke out into a smile, and stumbled forward on his hands and knees towards him, holding out his hand, wanting Lou to join them in their singing.

Lou had no intention of singing. But there was something they could help him with. And when else were they likely to be this jolly and conducive to being persuaded into something?

Lou crawled his way over to the two of them. They sat propped up against the back wall of the cart, sitting back to back with the driver, who sat slumped with the reins draping from his fingers. A bump in the road caught Lou just as he was righting himself and he fell flat on his face, bumping his nose against the bottom of the cart.

Poels and Eirk both let out a cheer, and then he felt their slightly drunken grip on his forearms, helping him to sit up there beside the two of them.

"Young Louson!" Poels said, his eyes gleaming in the twilight glow. "Whatcha been up ta, boy?"

The other working hands always addressed him by his full name. Just something he'd got used to. Lou steeled himself, forced a smile onto his lips.

Eirk clapped him on the back. "Another summer done, then, eh? Bet you're looking forward to tucking in this winter? Nothing much to do except drink and be merry!"

Eirk and Poels caught one another's eye and then began to belt out another of their songs. This one wasn't familiar to Lou, and he just waited it out, thinking to himself that soon they'd be arriving in Endmere and then he'd lose his opportunity. He needed to ask them. And he needed to do it right now.

Eirk lurched forward and grabbed hold of a chunk of Lou's

cheek and squeezed, right where his scar was. He pursed his lips and sucked in air. "Ooh, that's a nasty one. Real shiner, right? Dearie me, come to think of it I remember Junth Junior giving you that and all. Real wrong, that was, these young kids don't know they're even born."

Lou noticed that Poels wore an identical expression to Eirk, and he knew that this was his opportunity, while he had them in one of these melancholy dips of mood. He swallowed hard and met their drunken gaze. "Junth took my winter's supplement—told me that I'd shown him descent. And told me that if I come back next year he'll have the skuller hang, draw and quarter me."

This seemed to catch the two of them off guard. Eirk and Poels were both temporarily stunned by this comment, and Lou wondered whether he'd gone too far, if he hadn't dressed it up enough. He should've layered it on, about his family, his pa's job, how they'd *starve* that winter without the supplement.

Poels slapped Lou on the shoulder, and gave him a fatherly squeeze. "Tough luck, that one, son. Real tough luck."

Lou kept his stare steady, trying to keep his eyes on both Poels and Eirk at the same time. He was sure that if he could just maintain eye contact then he could convince them. That was the only option he had.

Eirk nodded along with his friend and leaned out over the cart, propping his elbow up on the side and peering out towards the back, to the road receding from them. "Remember when I was younger"—he turned back to look at Lou—"'bout your age, in fact, I got a pretty similar threat made to me." He smiled gently. "Never did go back there, that's the best thing to do in that situation, I reckon. Just cut your losses and find some more work."

"Yup, yup," Poels said, closing his eyes and pressing his lips together tightly.

Both of these men were going to be a real joy for their wives that evening.

Lou felt the light get brighter around them, and he turned just where he sat, looked out behind him, to where the cart was headed. There it was. The skuller's post which stood on the edge of town. On the edge of Endmere.

It was a fortification made of planks of wood—wood his pa had helped saw up and stick together, or so he'd told Lou—and it was lit with several dozen torches which flickered away, bathing the whole structure with an odd, intense yellow light. He eyed a pair of skullers who stood at the entrance, who lifted the door for the cart to pass through.

The structure extended around the whole of Endmere, forming an oval around the village, about ten or eleven feet high. Since Endmere was a small place, only around a hundred, maybe two hundred, inhabitants, there was only a small guard of skullers here. Perhaps four or five in all.

The skullers themselves came from the central outpost, several miles from here. Skullers in general kept themselves to themselves. Or it might've been the working at night that pushed them to the periphery of society.

The door dropped shut behind them, shutting with the clatter of wood on stone which echoed about the inside of the fort for several moments. Lou breathed in the familiar scents of his village. First there was that sewage smell, and he saw it running in the gutters, those mulchy brown rivulets streaming down, seemingly without end, headed out underneath the fort and far from the village. His pa, too, had worked on that. But that didn't matter now—now he was going to starve to death.

They all were.

The cart hit the cobblestones and the wheels bounced upon them. The horses' hooves clopped against the stone and Lou could already taste the stench of brandy wine and ale mixed in the air. He looked over to their tavern *The Mocker's Pit*, and saw that already people were hovering about outside.

They were other working hands who'd been working on other farms, and they'd come back a little earlier, got a head start on their drinking. It was tradition that after bringing in the yield the working hands would all drink themselves mad, but it was a tradition that Lou had never really understood.

And certainly never taken part in.

He wasn't like the other working hands. He didn't have the grung to fritter away like they did. He had to help put food on his table.

To his dismay, Lou noticed that Poels and Eirk were already waving off at their friends there, outside *The Mocker's*, calling out to them. Lou knew it was too late. But he had to try. His family were at stake and he wasn't a coward, that much he was sure of. He might be doughy, young and now jobless, but he had always believed himself to have a gut of steel.

Well, now was the time for him to show it.

The cart slowed and then ebbed to a halt at the saddling post. Lou glanced back to see the driver stepping down from the seat and going to tie up his horses. He wouldn't be able to leave Endmere till tomorrow. Not without a guard of skullers. And no common driver could afford to pay for that. It just wasn't economically feasible, which was to say nothing about safety. No, at night it was better to stay inside a fort, to put trust in the skullers.

Lou shifted to look to Eirk, who was already halfway across the cart, swaying from side to side as he walked, like a sturdy oak tree caught in a strong wind. Poels, though, hadn't left so quickly. In fact, he was still slumped up in the cart, holding his head and blinking hard every so often. Lou guessed that he had had a little too much to drink on the ride over.

Lou listened to the *stomp* as Eirk landed on the cobbles beneath the cart and then watched him waddle over to his friends. Poels just stayed right where he was, and the driver of the cart didn't look in much hurry to throw them out, he was busy with a bucket swinging from his hand, going to get water for the horses.

Lou propped himself up, then reached out and took hold of Poels's shoulder. He gripped him tight, feeling his fingernails digging into the man's tunic. Poels, though, didn't seem all that bothered by this, he just stared at some point in mid-air, apparently still trying to get his vision straight.

"Listen, please," Lou said, already feeling his voice shake a little. "My family's going to starve this winter without my supplement. I need grung." He stared more intently at Poels not sure whether or not the man was really hearing him. "Can you help me?"

Poels continued to stare into the space in front of him, and then he seemed to regain his consciousness. Slowly he turned and looked in Lou's direction. Blinked once, twice, then said, "How . . . how much you need?"

Lou felt his chest warm a little. He forced himself to smile. "Half the supplement would be okay, we could survive on it, maybe . . . I . . . I don't know. Whatever you can give."

Poels considered Lou for a moment or so longer and then dug his hand inside his tunic, to the pocket he had sewn inside. He pawed through it and then produced a pair of coins, some grung, and handed it over to Lou. He smiled drunkenly, his head bobbing all about, then reached up and gave Lou a slap on the shoulder.

He somehow staggered up to his feet and then swayed his way off the cart, almost tripping and falling as he reached the back end, but he finally got there. And then he leaped down and made his way across the square, zig-zagging his way over to his waiting friends, the other working hands, all of them drinking outside *The Mocker's*.

They cheered as he approached.

Lou pressed himself back into the cart, holding those two coins which Poels had given him. He looked down at the pair of them, at their dirty bronze faces. Two grung. Enough to get himself a flask of brandy wine and drink his troubles away. But not much more.

He looked out over the square, to *The Mocker's* and wondered whether having a drink wouldn't be such a bad idea. He could get rid of this all, if just for a little while. He could forget about his rotten day . . . no, the whole rotten season. What did it matter any more? He could spend the entirety of his wages and it wouldn't make any difference to his family's situation.

But something deep inside him told him that it would be wrong. That he couldn't give up so willingly. He had to fight just a little longer if he could. Something would come up, or he'd think of something.

He was sure of it.

He got up from the cart and then beat a hasty retreat for his house, taking a back alley so he didn't need to walk past the front of *The Mocker's*, and the other working hands drinking there.

He knew that Poels might well tell them that he'd asked for money, those working hands would tell their wives, and pretty soon the whole town would know. It had been a great mistake. But now he'd made the mistake there was nothing he could about it.

Nothing at all.

5

BACK HOME

LOU WOKE UP the next morning with the sun in his face. It was a strange feeling. Most mornings this summer he'd been accustomed to getting up well before dawn, getting himself ready for when the cart headed out to Old Man Junth's farm. But today he had no need to get up, and his body had seemed to know it too, allowing him to sleep in.

He felt the sun rays warming up his bed sheets. He turned on his side so the light wouldn't shine right in his eyes. He could smell a faint scent of bacon and, the crackling of the grease. He knew that soon his ma would be serving breakfast. He recalled all these mornings he'd had, the day after he'd brought in the yield. Every last one of them he'd got himself up, almost leaped up out of bed, with a smile on his face, feeling like a prince. But now, today, this morning, he felt thoroughly depressed.

Sleeping on the problem hadn't provided any solution. He had run everything through his mind. He'd thought of getting his pa to spread his net a little, for him to get out into the next village along to look for more work. But that idea had died on its feet when he'd remembered that Pa wasn't a member of the Guild, and if he wanted to join he would have to pay the yearly fee. And that would've taken a hefty chunk out of Lou's wages, a chunk that they simply couldn't afford.

His ma might also spread her medicine services in some villages around the area, but he had noticed that cough of hers, those dark shadows beneath her eyes, and he got the feeling that she might well be on the doorstep of some fever. And the last thing they needed with winter coming was for his ma to get ill. The nights would get longer and travel to find medicine would be almost impossible. And that was to say nothing for the travel expenses themselves.

His little sis Syre hadn't much to give. She was only ten years old, and buried in her books. She could hardly lift a wedge of wood, let alone an axe. No, if he was to keep his family from starving this winter then *he* would have to do something. It was his responsibility, after all, he'd been the one who'd got his winter's supplement taken away from him. And now he'd let the whole town know just how hard up they were. It'd be his responsibility to put things right again.

As he got up out of bed, shucking his bed sheet, letting it tumble into a pile on the floor, he felt his muscles drawn all tight, and that weariness sink over him. He knew that was his body telling him that he'd slept on for too long, that he was messing up his body's routine. His body expected for him to go out to Old Man Junth's again that day, and it was aching and complaining. He wished he could tell it that it could rest all it liked from now on, but that it might not be around to see the next spring.

That scent of bacon got richer, thicker. He felt his stomach tremble at the prospect of those crunchy rashers in his mouth. Saliva seeped out and covered his tongue. Those crackles seemed to get louder still. As he got dressed, putting on a fresh tunic his ma had hung up by his door, he smelled the gentle burning smell of bread, and that stench of warm butter.

Perhaps he would see things better after a hearty breakfast.

The tunic was soft against his skin. His ma used some special herbs of hers to get it like this, to get it to smell so clean and sharp too. He loved that smell, and he pressed the material over his mouth and nostrils and breathed it right in. It reminded him of when he'd been a young boy, and there'd be a storm raging, or something, and he'd just collect his bed sheets up in a ball in his fist and he'd smell it hard, and that'd make him feel better.

Braver.

Now he needed all the bravery he could get.

He staggered through the house, his muscles locking up on him about a dozen times, finally making it through to the kitchen, where he drew up the hobbledy chair made of cast-off wood. His pa had made it a good decade or so ago, when Lou had been seven or eight. He remembered standing over him, watching him do it. The sawdust flying into the air, catching those flakes on his tongue till Pa had told him to stop, that he'd get sick if he swallowed any.

The only one in the kitchen was Ma. She stood over at the stove, her white apron tied up around her waist. It had lots of stains on it now, all kinds of fruit juices, some butter, bacon grease. Whenever she washed it, it just seemed to get dirty all over again, so Lou didn't see the reason in her washing it in the first place.

Her hair stuck up in frayed strands, and her face was all red, hot and bothered. She wiped her brow with the back of her hand as she worked, but when she turned to look at Lou over her shoulder, she managed a smile. "You were off to bed quick last night."

Lou smiled faintly. "Yeah, I was pretty tired, I guess."

She turned back to the stove. "A day of bringing in the yield'll do that to you."

"Yup."

She stirred away at something, and then called out, into the house, "Fenklow! Fenklow!"

Fenklow was his pa's name. His pa always liked to sleep in in the mornings. Although Lou would never say so much out loud, he knew that his pa was getting old, and he was beginning to need his rest. Perhaps if his pa got himself out of bed a little earlier he'd find more carpentry work in the village, but, at the same time, Lou couldn't think of his pa ruining his health just for the sake of a few more grung.

Now, though, maybe he'd have to.

They'd need to scrap together all the grung they could get.

"Fenklow, breakfast's ready!"

Lou heard footsteps out in the hall, but he knew, without even looking up to the doorway, that they didn't belong to his pa. It was his little sis, Syre. She was rubbing the sleep from her eyes, still half-stunned from her dreaming. She pulled up the chair beside Lou, making the feet scrape against the floor as she did so.

Ma twizzled round from the stove. "You take care with that floor, you hear? Gotta take care of this place, gonna last you and Louson the whole your lives if you take care of it right."

Syre rested her chin on her arm and cast a glance across the table at Lou, rolling her eyes slightly.

Lou found himself chuckling, just a little. They always had

that private joke between the two of them, that thing that Ma always said. It felt good to laugh, just a little went a long way.

His ma spun round from the stove, wooden spatula in hand, and she wagged it at them. "You two had better not be talking behind my back."

"We didn't say anything, Ma," Lou said, knowing that in essence he was telling the truth.

His ma glowered at the both of them then turned back to the stove, dishing out the crispy bacon and eggs, piling it on top of the buttered toast on a pair of clay plates with a slight *tinkle*. Then she spun right round and bellowed out into the house one more time. "Fenklow! You get here right now or I'll feed this to the first mongrel dog that so much as sniffs at our porch!"

In that moment, just sitting here in the kitchen, Lou could almost forget his problems, his family's problems. But each time he felt his mind getting away from the matter, it just came right back, snapping at him like one of those cursed rabbits that hopped through the countryside at night.

They all ate their breakfast in silence, like always. Perhaps silence wasn't the right word, though. Lou liked to think more of it as pigs all collected round a trough at dinner time. And that was ironic seeing as they were eating bacon. Everyone, his ma, pa and sis, all had their snouts down at their plate, mopping up their egg yolks with their toast and crunching on their rashers of bacon.

Soon after taking the first bite, Lou had realised he wasn't all that hungry. The first time he'd not had an appetite at breakfast. And since then he'd forced his own breakfast down himself, not bothering to listen to those nauseous surges pounding through him. He knew just what those feelings meant, though. He knew that he *had* to tell his parents what was wrong.

Or else they'd hear off some neighbour that he'd been asking round for money. And that would be embarrassing beyond words.

He waited till his ma had collected up all their plates and thrown them into the washing-up tub, then, just as she was wiping her hands clean on her apron, he picked his moment. He eyed his sis and pa, both of them readying to get up from their seats, getting ready to go about their days.

"Everybody," Lou said, already feeling his tonsils red raw, and his breakfast churning away in his stomach. "I've got something that I've gotta tell you."

He watched his pa and sis exchange glances, then retake their seats. His pa was wearing his work tunic and a pair of ragged old trousers, all a faded mud-brown colour.

His sis had on her billowy yellow dress for school, and a matching ribbon in her hazelnut-coloured hair.

Both their eyes lingered on him, and he noticed the look of surprise there. Lou guessed that he must've looked more grave-faced than he'd imagined. He got himself paranoid thinking that they might already know what he was about to say. But he reminded himself that it was impossible.

"It's to do with my winter's supplement," Lou said.

His pa scratched his balding scalp, his fingernails scraping against his dried skin, making flakes rise up in the air, into the sunbeams which burst in through the kitchen windows. "What about your winter's supplement?"

Lou looked to his ma, now resting up against the stove, her

expression vacant, her lips bloodless. He couldn't put this off any longer. He had to tell them the truth. Just like it'd happened.

"Well," Lou said, feeling a mixture of hysteria and relief, the tightness growing across his chest, and that salty, greasy taste of bacon almost getting lost in his numbing mouth, "I didn't get it."

The room drifted into silence.

His words seemed to hang there, between them all, smothering everybody.

Bird chirping sounded outside the kitchen window, and the noises out in the street seemed to grow louder. There was a cartwheel turning, hooves clacking out against the cobblestones, some seller was jibbing through his sales patter.

Lou looked over his family's faces, those stone expressions. They knew what it meant. There was no reason for him to tell them. They knew just how badly they were in trouble, that they would *starve* this coming winter.

His pa, his lips quivering slightly, laid his calloused hand on the table. Lou stared at those battered, yellowing fingernails, and he thought of all the work he'd done in his life, all those blisters now part of the patchwork of his skin. The man most likely had wood shavings in his bloodstream. "Well," his pa said, "I guess we're just gonna have to think of something."

His ma, too, seemed to gradually return from shock. "Nothing else for it."

Lou felt his mind drifting away from him, his throat got drier and it got hard to breathe.

Lou could only pull in a tiny mouthful of air at a time. He reached down and grasped the seat of his chair, feeling that sturdy wood in his grip made him feel better somewhat. When he spoke it was like his voice just withered and died in his throat. "But what," Lou said, "what're we gonna do? You know we can't survive without the supplement."

He paused, the next words sticking in his throat. Now he'd dropped this gigantic boulder right into the middle of all their lives, he wasn't sure whether he could really add another. But maybe it was just better to get everything out all at once. Put everything on the table. And so he straightened up and forced himself to take a deep breath. "There's something else," he said. "Old Man Junth says I'm not to come back the next year."

"What?" his pa said, frowning. "Why's that?"

"Well," Lou replied, "actually, you see, the thing is that his son, Herbert Junth, he's just taken over the running of the farm. And he didn't like something I did, earlier on in the season, said I don't know how to follow orders or something like it. Anyway, upshot of the thing is that he won't let me come back next year. If we make it through winter I'll have to look for another farm, another place, I—"

His pa held up his hand. "Yes, yes, we'll cross that bridge when we get to it, but right now we've gotta think about how we're gonna get through this winter, here. Way things are, what we've got, we'll have no grung for food."

Lou swallowed hard and pressed his back against his chair.

For whatever he thought about his pa growing older and weaker, he could still quite easily silence him when he wanted. He was the head of the family, after all. And he made the decisions around here.

"Now, way I see it," Pa continued, "we've only really got one option, and that's for us to go looking for work this winter—"

Syre rose off her chair, making the feet screech against the kitchen floor, and glared at him. "But what about my schooling?"

Pa held up his hand again for silence. He shook his head. "It'd be a damn shame but sometimes we've gotta make priorities. And sometimes that means that schooling comes after." He shook his head again at Syre as she opened her mouth to protest again. "It doesn't matter about your complaining, now, because you've gotta remember that without food in your belly you're nothing, nothing at all. And there ain't much point filling your brain full of books if you're just gonna be a corpse at the end of it, is there?"

Syre stayed silent.

Pa jabbed his finger down on the table. "Now, listen here, this is what we're gonna do now, you all listening to me? First off, I'm gonna get talking with some of the men from the Guild, see if there's anything I might—"

"Pa," Lou said, doing something that he almost never did— interrupt his pa. "That's gonna cost money, and there's no way that we could do that. Even say you did straighten things out fine with the Guild, what's to say you'd find work in the other villages? They might already have enough carpenters there. From what I've heard there's some working hands that work at carpentry in the winters."

His pa shook his head and curled his lip. "Those damn greedy vermin, they are. Can't let a decent man have his occupation, earn his bread."

Lou just sat in his chair, staring at the wood grain of the table, thinking to himself. His mind felt wrapped up in a loop, the same old thoughts just drifting right back to him the whole time. He had never been any good at carpentry, or anything, really. Farming was all he knew.

Being a working hand.

He could put in a day's graft and that was just about all he was good for. He was in his early twenties, and he thought of the other boys in the village, the ones he'd grown up with.

Most of them had left now.

They'd learned a skill then settled somewhere nearby. Others had settled here, in the village. They were bakers or blacksmiths or carpenters just like his pa.

But Lou, he had nothing. Nothing but his dumb strength and shire-horse stubbornness. All the stubbornness and strength in the world would be no good if there was no food to put on the table. He'd die just like any other person.

When he glanced up, he saw that his pa was staring right at him, a distant look in his eye. "There is one thing that you might think of doing, son."

"Oh, yeah?" Lou said, his voice shrivelling up in his throat. "And what's that?"

"You ever thought about training up as a skuller?"

6

ENTERING THE TRADE

T HE FORT was cleared at this time, in the early evening. The sun was just looming on the horizon, about ready to dip down, to drape night all across the landscape. Soon the animals would return. Soon the skullers would be required.

Lou tried to clear his mind of those thoughts. He had one thing and one thing only on his mind, and that was that he simply *had* to be accepted. If he wasn't then his family would starve, and it would be all his fault.

He felt the warmth in the earth coming up at him, and could hear, inside the hut which stood alongside the fort, the several gravelly voices from within. He knew that was the dormitory, that was where the out-of-town skullers slept during the day. Before long they would be out on the forts, prowling along, looking for any threat to Endmere.

He could still taste his ma's broth in his mouth, the thick saltiness of it, and the rich scent of the potatoes continued to hang in his nostrils. That was what he concentrated on as he stepped over a sewage channel, eyeing the hut a little further along, which was known to be where the head skuller, Murch, lived.

Murch had lived in Endmere for decades. Lou's parents told him that he'd shown up the day they'd built the fort around the village to serve as head skuller. He'd been around since before Lou had been born. Murch was never seen about the village, in the square, or out buying his vegetables or freshly caught rabbits for stew, or trout caught down in the nearby stream for grilling.

And so something of a myth had sprung up about him, and Lou admitted to himself that he secretly feared Murch just like everyone else.

Lou felt his boots weighing his feet down as he walked up to the ragged wooden doors of the hut and rapped his fist against it twice.

Sounds of stirring came from inside. The odd uttered swearword. And then there was a *clatter* followed by a *splash*, the sound of a bucket of water being overturned, or so Lou imagined. More swearing and then Lou felt footsteps pound through the ground, sending a shudder up his spine.

The door whipped back. Its hinge groaned in protest. For a couple of moments Lou could only make out the gloominess inside. He couldn't make out any shapes. And then Murch stepped forward, into the fading light of the day. He snorted long and hard then wiped his nose with his hand. "Wha'tha hell you want?"

Murch was a short man, but he was thick too. His chest was incredibly wide, and rippled with muscles, even though the tunic he wore, the one he'd been sleeping in, was pretty loose fitting.

His width carried on down right to his waist, to his tremendous gut which hung down limp. There was a large scar right from his left eye reaching all the way down to the point of his chin. At certain points it got wider, the skin got rawer, and Lou thought it looked a bit like a valley.

Murch glared at him and rubbed his head with his bulging fingers. He had wiry black hair growing over the backs of his knuckles and his skin was leathery, hard, a little like Lou's pa's hands, but more so.

It was clear that Murch had earned that skin in combat, not sanding down wood.

Lou felt his whole body get caught in a shudder. He ground his teeth and sucked air in, trying to clear his head, to get right just what he'd come here to do. There was no turning back now. "I . . . I, uh—"

"Go on, then, out with it already!"

This time Lou got himself more together, managed to at least keep his voice steady. "I was wondering if I could join the skullers."

Musk wafted out from inside the hut, it was stringent, unbearable, and it mixed up with the sewage stream running not too far away. It got into Lou's lungs, thoroughly rinsing them clean of any remainder of his dinner, of the smells and tastes of the broth.

The feeling was so stifling that he could almost feel bile rising in his throat.

Murch closed one eye and peered at Lou with his opened one. "Wha'dya think you're doing coming out here, so early and all?"

"Early?" Lou said. "It's almost night time."

Murch sneered at him, showing off his yellowed teeth, several of them with chunks of meat still stuck between them, from whatever he'd eaten before going to bed. Murch snorted again, and then, hocked up a great load of phlegm and spat it out into the dust at Lou's feet.

Lou felt some of the spittle splash against the leg of his trousers. It was a green-brown colour, and thick as honey. But he forced himself not to think about it. He jerked his head back up and forced himself to meet Murch's eye. "What do I need to do to join?" Lou said.

"Eh?"

"To join the skullers."

Murch flinched at this with apparent disgust. Then he glanced over Lou a second time. Slowly a smile formed on his lips, and then a deep, throaty laugh sounded deep within him.

It sent a chill passing through Lou. That sound was wretched. Even worse than the sound of him spitting. But he stood firm and waited.

Murch shook his head from side to side, still gathering himself from his laughter. As his smile faded, he caught Lou's eye. "What d'ya think, that you can just show up and we'll give you a uniform, a sword, a crossbow, let you join in?"

Now that he said it, it sounded so ridiculous to Lou. This whole idea had been stupid from the start. He knew his pa had been speaking out of desperation, and that this would never come off. Not in a million years. Everything about it was wrong.

"Right," Lou said, turning to go. He was resolved to think of something, something better. His family's lives were at stake and so what else *could* he do? He had to find something, somewhere he could get paid.

"Wait," Murch said.

Lou hesitated, meeting his eye again.

Murch sniffed again then scratched his arse. That sly smile of his was back again, but thankfully he wasn't laughing. "You're a farm boy, aintcha?"

"A working hand."

Murch shrugged as if he didn't care about the difference, though to Lou there was a big one. Where a farm boy grew up on a farm, in a family which owned a farm, a working hand was just as it sounded. Someone to pay to come along and do the grunt work from spring to summer.

Herbert Junth was a *farm boy*.

"So whatcha doin' here then, messing about with skullers? Your winter's supplement not enough for you, or what?" He snorted again. "You do realise that skullers get killed—all the time round here. And it ain't no noble death if that's what you're thinking." He narrowed his eyes. "When you get thems animals' poison into them veins of yours there ain't nothing even your ma can do to help."

Lou wanted to pummel the man for that, bringing his ma into this. She had nothing at all to do with it. Though, thinking it about it some more, he supposed the reason he'd got so riled about it was because of the fact that Murch even knew what his ma did for a living. That she dabbled in medicine.

Murch was like a shadow at night, no one ever saw him around, no one thought of him as being part of the community even. And so, Lou guessed, they all just believed that he knew as little about their lives as they did about his.

Not so true, it turned out.

Murch hocked up phlegm again, readying himself to spit a second time. Then, apparently catching Lou's expression, he stopped himself, grinned that broad, deep grin of his again, that scar running down the side of his face opening wider as he did. "You know what, you're not so bad-looking for a skuller."

Lou's heart bobbed up to his throat. It was like someone had slapped him hard on the back. "Really?"

Murch pouted. "Yeah, really. You're a big guy." He tilted his head to one side. "Bit soft here and there but we'll soon sort that out with some training."

It was like Lou felt his feet lifting off the ground, like he was floating in the air. He had to use all the will in his body to prevent himself from smiling. He had to stay serious. This was his chance and he couldn't say or do anything *stupid* that would rob him of it.

"Yeah," Murch said, nodding to himself. "Think we can work with you." He looked Lou over a final time, like a merchant checking out a horse on sale, then he met Lou's gaze long and hard, and whatever warm glow of optimism had been glowing inside of Lou was suddenly extinguished. "You do realise the dangers, dontcha, kid? This ain't no game."

Lou kept himself still, as still as he could. He thought of his ma, his pa, his sis. This was for them. "What's the pay like?"

Murch's pout finally cracked and a long, broad smile passed over his lips. "You'll fit right in here, fella, I'm tellin' ya.

"You'll be just fine."

It turned out that Lou would get paid a hundred grung a week as a junior skuller. That was the same that he'd earn in a month as a working hand. And the work was year round. If Lou worked hard, made his bones and passed up to the full rank of skuller, then he'd be paid two hundred and fifty grung a week, which was more grung than he knew what to do with.

In only a month of working as a skuller he would earn a thousand grung: his entire winter's supplement and then some. But even if he stayed on as a junior skuller he would still earn his winter's supplement back in ten weeks. It seemed that all his family's problems were solved. There would be food on the table this winter.

Just as long as he could keep the job

... and stay alive.

Murch first took him to what he called the 'tool shed' and fitted him out with a skuller's uniform. It was just like the ones that Lou had seen his whole life, and it was strange to find himself confronted with it now. He reached out to stroke the rugged, jet-black fabric, and he felt its roughness beneath his fingertips.

He could feel Murch standing on his shoulder, breathing all over him, that sour breath of his, with a slight tinge of blood there. When Lou got a better look inside Murch's mouth on their way to the tool shed he'd seen that he'd been missing several teeth, and others were crooked or cracked. Lou wondered what his mouth might look like after serving as a skuller for a year or more: the minimum length of his contract as junior skuller.

Lou tugged the uniform off its rusty nail and held it out before him. It was heavy, a hard fabric, and he knew that it was designed to be that way, so that if he got bitten by an animal, if the skuller was lucky, the fangs wouldn't make it through.

But Lou had seen the bodies at dawn, covered in the sable sheets. Once they had even taken one with them on their cart as far as the next village over.

Still, to this day, he couldn't shake that rancid stench of death that had hung about that corpse.

The uniform had a hood, too. Perhaps that was to help him stay hidden. To ward the animals off.

Murch's breath warmed his neck, and then he said, "Well come on, then, put it on. There's work to be done, my lad. We're needed up on the fort."

Lou pulled the uniform down over his head, poking his head out through the hole. He pulled the hood down off his head.

Murch smiled. "You'll need that hood round dawn, I'm telling you, my boy. Wouldn't want to catch a death. That gets just as many skullers as the animals."

Lou flattened the creases out of his uniform and then glanced to the other wall of the tool shed, where the various weapons hung. He picked out the crossbows, all of them seemingly identical, their mechanisms well-oiled, sheening slightly with the moonlight that got in through the gaps in the wooden-plank walls.

Murch rested his hand on Lou's shoulder. His breath only seemed to get worse. To get hotter and hotter, fouler and fouler. "Go on then, lad, you take your pick. All as like as one another not to make much of a difference."

Lou took him at his word and slipped the crossbow nearest to him off its nail, and then passed the strap over his shoulder, just like he'd always seen the other skullers do. He felt its steady weight on him, the bolts there too, snug in the pouch beneath the crossbow.

Murch turned to the other wall, and Lou turned with him.

There were the swords. Dozens of them, all hanging from their hilts.

Their blades were a dull grey, covered in pockmarks of earlier battles. The handles, too, were covered in stained bandages—bandages that had once been white but were now stained with sooty marks.

Ingrained sweat.

Murch took one of the swords indiscriminately and then one of the sheaths that hung down below. The sheaths weren't fine either, all of them seemed to consist of cast-off cloth all bundled together, and, like the handles of the blades themselves, were covered with sooty marks.

Fully kitted-out now, Murch stood back and gave Lou a smirk. "Looks like you're ready for a night out on the fort."

Lou felt his strength fully tested with the weight of this load. The sword was the worst part, the way it kept causing his waistline to slip, and how he had to keep hoiking his trousers back up.

Murch chuckled. "Dontcha worry about that. Skullers soon learn to wear big hulking belts." He flipped up the hem of his tunic to show him that, indeed, he had a thick, woven leather belt from which to hang a sword. He let the hem of his tunic fall back down then said, "If you're ready then we'll go."

THE NIGHT WATCH

LOU FELT his hands quickly growing stiff from the cold up on the fort. He felt someone tap him on the arm and he looked to see another of the skullers, Sulliman, as he'd introduced himself, holding out a pair of battered, but hardy-looking, leather gloves.

Lou shuddered as he dragged the gloves onto his hands. He felt the velvety insides of them, the soft material up against his skin, and he instantly felt warmer. He looked back at Sulliman, or Sully as he'd told him to call him.

Murch had appointed Sully, as fully-fledged skuller, to keep an eye on Lou.

Sully was a wiry man, in his late-thirties or thereabouts. He had neck-long, jet-black hair, and seemingly matching eyes. At all times he kept his hand resting on the hilt of his sword, as if one of the cursed animals might leap him from behind, even up here on the battlements.

Lou wondered if Sully was just being paranoid or whether he had a real concern about it. In any case, this being his first night, he felt himself on edge.

Lou smiled gently. "Thanks," he said, nodding to the leather gloves now snug on his hands.

Sully winked. "The boss always seems to forget something with the new recruits. Although sometimes I wonder if he does it on purpose just to test them out, like."

Lou gave him a nod.

Sully rested his elbows on the rim of the wooden fort and stared out into the gloomy plains before them.

The plains were set in total darkness now except for the odd torch providing a burning glow, a small patch of light. There was nothing to see out there right at the moment, but Lou well knew that perception didn't mean anything. He had grown up his entire life keeping his ears primed to any sound out in the darkness, to the snapping of a twig, the rustle of leaves in the trees, or the cracking of a branch under foot.

His stomach heaved a little as he looked out over the plains, that hearty broth of his ma's seemingly a long way off now, its reassuring warm, salty scent miles away from the brisk night air up here on the fort. But he knew that he had to be here, that he had to man the fort if his family were to survive the winter.

Sully hadn't batted an eyelid as he'd reeled through his own story. It was frighteningly similar to Lou's, really. Just like him, Sully had been a working hand and, just like Lou, he'd been turned out by the farmer, told not to come back. And, it seemed, that farmer had taken the trouble to rouse the suspicion that Sully was a trouble-maker throughout the farms about the place.

When he'd returned the next season to look for work he'd found himself turned away everywhere he asked.

After several nights out on the streets of Endmere, begging for crumbs from the late-night drinkers in *The Mocker's Pit* he'd gone a knocking on Murch's door, just like Lou had. And Murch had been glad to take him on.

And so here he was, a skuller.

It wasn't a bad living, or so he said to Lou. Although they'd only just met, Lou noticed that he seemed to bring up the subject of pay several times over, telling him that another five years of this and he'd be off somewhere, go and buy himself some land and start up his own farm. Once he could afford the protection of his own skullers, of course.

That was the main obstacle facing most of the farmers, and why there were so few of them. Only those with the biggest operations could really make it pay. The ones who could afford the skullers' protection.

When Sully breathed in and out, he made a slight rasping sound at the back of his throat, like he had a perpetual cold. He clasped his hands together and kept on staring out into the darkness, then he said, in a low voice, "You ever wonder what all this was like before?"

"Before what?" Lou said.

Sully turned to face him. "You know, before the plains were roaming with these cursed animals? Before, when it was safe to go out at night?"

"Don't you remember?"

Sully shook his head. "Nah, I was only wee when the curse was cast. Maybe five or six." He smiled a little. "Ever since I can remember it's been just like this, we've been afraid to go out at night."

Lou stared out into the darkness with him. He focussed on a flickering torch, just a little off in the distance, about a hundred yards from the fortification. For several moments he found himself hypnotised by the glare, the brightness of the light. And then some motion caught the corner of his eye.

He jerked his head round to look.

Were his eyes playing tricks on him or had he just seen something, moving there?

He squinted and stared hard into that space of blackness.

"You see something, fella?" Sully said, a slight hop of excitement in his voice.

Lou continued to stare, trying to strip back the darkness, to see down there, to make out the shape of whatever it was. And then he caught it, saw the motion. It was coming toward them, and fast.

As it drew closer and Lou's eyes got more and more accustomed, he realised it was a sheep.

A rampaging sheep.

He slipped Sully an urgent sidelong glance, but before he'd even caught up with what was going on, he saw Sully there, holding his crossbow in his arms, both of them at perfect right angles with one another, and then the bolt zipped out into the darkness.

Lou heard it hit.

It made a meaty, *thwack*.

He peered down there, trying to strip back the darkness, to see the form again. It was more difficult now, impossible even. His eyes were much better at tracking motion in the darkness, but still objects, not so much. It took Sully pointing off in the direction of his shot, only ten or twenty yards or so from the fort, to the carcass lying there.

Lou saw it now, just on the periphery of their glowing torches.

The sheep's body lay completely still, the bolt sticking out from its neck.

Lou glanced round at Sully. "How'd you ever get to be such a good shot?"

Sully gave him a faint grin. "Practice," he said. "Lots of practice."

As they made their way down the fort to retrieve the carcass, Sully seemed to grow slightly twitchy. He glanced up at another of the skullers, a little way off along the fort, and gave him an odd sort of salute, sticking his thumb, middle finger and little finger out, before continuing on his way, Lou at his side.

"What was that about?" Lou said.

"Signalling a kill," Sully said. "Telling them to stay on their guard." Sully held his crossbow out before him, still crutched in his hands, his eyes primed, peeling back the darkness about them. "A dead one's got a knack of bringing others from nearby." He glanced briefly at Lou. "It's like the smell of blood brings them all in." He turned back to the darkness, continuing his prowl with the crossbow. "So it's better to remove the carcasses right away. Wouldn't want to bring a bunch of them here. Especially not something bigger. Wolves, bears, something like that. Might be more than the defences can handle."

Lou felt a tingle go right up his spine. All the bones in his body seemed to jangle. Ever since he'd been a boy he'd always supposed that the skullers were some kind of insuperable force, that they could easily hold off the animals. That was the only reason he'd been able to sleep at night, knowing they were safe.

And now that had been shattered.

They trudged on. Lou felt the brush of the long plain grass against his trouser leg. Already he could smell that sharp scent of the animal. The blood wafting up in the air. He glanced about, growing increasingly more uncertain by the second, worrying that something else might jump out at them.

As they drew closer to the sheep carcass, Lou got a scent of that mutton scent, the sharp animal musk. It reminded him of all those shanks of mutton they'd had in his house, that his ma had served piping hot alongside boiled potatoes, seasoned so as to send that meaty taste to the back of his mouth. Now, though, it was right at the front of his mouth.

And so strong as to almost overpower him.

He listened to Sully's steady bootfall as he kept his crossbow levelled in his hands, never for a second looking to the ground like Lou did, always aware of just what was going on around him, his head jerking off in all directions when he heard any sound.

Only then did Lou remember himself and pull out his own crossbow, set it in his own hands, and slip a bolt into the sling. He guessed that Sully hadn't thought to remind him thinking that a rookie skuller who had no idea how to handle a crossbow was just about as dangerous as a cursed animal.

But Lou had to do something.

He could hardly stand about leaving Sully uncovered while he looked over the carcass of the sheep. He had signed up to do his duty and so that was what he'd do.

Sully glanced round another time, then signalled back to the fort with that same three-fingered salute. In the distance, Lou saw that shadowy figure up on the fort return the gesture then set himself up against the wall, his own crossbow primed, covering them from any impending danger out on the plains.

Sully spoke out of the corner of his mouth, the only time his speech had been anything but steady and measured. Now it was almost hurried. "Keep an eye out, yeah?"

Lou did as he was told. He stared out around them, but couldn't see anything at all. The torches burning away, keeping up that flickering glow worked against him so that although he could see perfectly well in the near distance, he was near enough blind any further away.

He guessed what the skuller back at the fort covering them was for. He was keeping watch over that further distance. Lou guessed his job was one of a failsafe. If a cursed animal managed to escape the skuller's fire then it would be down to him to take the animal out at close range. Just as he was thinking that over, Sully crouched down over the dead animal, and said, "You might want your sword right about now."

Lou shouldered his crossbow once again, then grabbed for his sword. He listened to that dull scrape as he pulled it from its sheath and held it in his hand. It was so heavy that he staggered to one side before finding his balance.

Sully let out a dry chuckle. "Don't worry about that. Happens to all of us first time we take hold of the sword. You'll be fine from now on, though, dontcha worry."

Lou did feel stronger-footed now. He grasped the hilt of the sword tighter. He remembered all the sayings he'd heard down the years, all the bits and pieces of advice that'd been passed on third-hand as he'd worked the fields. That it was all about keeping your back straight, keeping the blade level with your nose, and when it came to swinging you had to swing back first to get a proper blow in. There was so much to keep in mind and Lou was afraid he'd just about forgotten it all in that moment.

Lou chanced a few glances back at Sully.

Sully worked quickly. He produced some bindings from the pocket of his trousers and set about tying up the legs of the sheep. That slight drag still sounded at the back of Sully's throat, the beginning of a cold. But he just snorted it back, in a similar way to how Murch had done earlier, and then stayed busy about his work. Soon enough he was ready. He glanced up to Lou with a wry grin, then said, "Back to the fort now."

On the way back, Lou kept turning backwards, facing off into the darkness, looking out there for anything trying to sneak up on them. But there was nothing. And he felt the tension in his muscles eek away.

Almost safe.

Almost back in Endmere, behind the fort again.

When the wooden gate dropped shut behind them with a *thunk*, Lou couldn't help but realise that this was the first time he'd ever returned to Endmere and not felt a hundred-per-cent safe.

He recalled how before whenever he'd come in after a day in the fields, beaten the approaching darkness, he'd always held his breath for the last few yards before they passed through the gate to the village. Only exhaling when he'd get inside, hear that familiar *thunk* of the gate closing behind them.

But this time it was different.

What Sully had said continued to play on his mind, that there were bigger animals out there, that there were animals that could overrun the defences. And only then did he realise what a charmed life he'd been leading.

Never before had he realised that his life might be hanging by such a precarious thread.

Another skuller, different from the one who'd signalled to Sully up on the fort, stepped down the narrow, rickety ladder that led up to the ramparts of the fort.

He was bulky, about the shape of a cannonball, and he walked with a slight wiggle. What marked him out from the other skullers was his light blond hair, and his bright blue eyes.

All the rest of the skullers had dark, sharp features, and were generally scrawny or had tight muscles.

The other thing which made him look different to the rest was his unsuppressible grin, splitting his rosy cheeks apart. He glanced over the sheep that Sully carried. "Good kill that one, saw you hitting it. Came right out of the dark, it did."

Sully smiled wanly, then dropped the carcass on the ground, several yards from the inside of the fort wall, and then he set about peeling out a battered cloth sack, shaking it clear of dust.

The smiley skuller nudged Lou in the ribs. "You're new about here, aintcha?"

Lou nodded.

"And Sully's takin' good care of you, is he?"

Again, Lou nodded.

"Got a voice on you, or what?"

". . . Yes," Lou said, his throat feeling dry, and his heart lapping at his tonsils.

The smiley skuller looked to Sully, wrinkled his brow, then

turned back to Lou. He gave him a half-smile. "Come on then, what sort of stories has he been tellin' ya?"

Lou felt his muscles lock up. He looked to Sully, straight-faced as he saw to the sheep, caking it with mud now out of a trough by his side. He was covering the whole corpse, smothering it with the stuff.

Only a second or so later did Lou realise it wasn't mud at all. It was cowpat.

That thick stench caught in his nostrils and turned his stomach another couple of degrees, crunching in on his dinner just a little more.

The smiley skuller, apparently unmoved by what Sully was doing, continued, "Yeah, Sully here, he likes to play with the rook-ies, scared their wits off and all that. He tell you that he thinks we're gonna get overrun by a bunch of cursed wolves or bears, summat like that?"

Lou felt the tension ebb out of his shoulders. And only then did he realise he'd been squeezing the hilt of his sword tight ever since he'd sheathed it, as they'd passed beneath the bridge. He released his grip and wiggled his fingers, trying to loosen the pent-up tension from them. He even managed a slight smile. "Yeah," Lou said. "He said something about wolves."

Sully just kept on working, silently smothering that cowpat into the sheep's carcass.

Lou saw that he'd put on a special pair of gloves over his regular ones. And he saw those gloves were caked with the stuff.

The smiley skuller held his hand out to Lou. "Name's Rutter-ness, but everyone calls me Rut."

Lou took his hand. It was strange shaking someone's hands while wearing gloves, but he did his best, listening to that slight *creak* of the leather on leather. "You're not from round here, are you?" Lou said.

Rut shook his head. "Nah, I'm from a few villages over. Quagsmile." He jerked his thumb in the direction of the dormitory shed. "Sleep in there at the moment, while I'm posted here, anyway."

Even in the cold night there was a thin layer of sweat gleaming on Rut's forehead. He wiped it away with the back of his gloved hand. "Joined up the skullers a while ago now. Worked the fields a few years, like most of us do, then figured it was a fools' game. This," he said, indicating the fort above him, "this is a proper job. Get good pay, see some action. Only problem really's the hours. Not the most social occupation in the world, if you catch my drift?"

Lou thought about how he'd been playing this fools' game for about the same time as Rut, till he'd come along here tonight and joined the skullers.

Rut grinned again, then gave Lou a slap on his upper arm. "You'll do fine enough," Rut said, turning to head back up the ladder, to go back up onto the fort. "He's a good man, Sully. Take care of you."

When Sully had finished, he looked over his work, the sheep now reduced to one great big block of moulded together cowpat, then he turned to Lou and said, "You wanna hold the sack open for me?"

Once they'd got the sheep in its bag, and that stench of manure still ringing through the whole of Lou's skull, or so it seemed, they went out to the back of the village and piled it right up on top of another bunch of sacks. Sacks which Lou supposed contained other animals too. More sheep, pigs or whatever other cursed animals had got in range of Endmere and had to be taken care of.

Sully ditched the over-sized gloves, dumping them beside the pile of bags. He sniffed and then looked to Lou. "Heading out again tonight."

"What?" Lou said, feeling a little stunned. He'd thought that their going out onto the plains, going out to pick up the carcass had been something that only happened once in a while, and that while he might have to do something like that again, he'd never dreamed he would have to go out again *tonight*.

"Gotta go check on the outpost, a couple of torches over. Strange that something that big would get through without being taken down by the skullers out on the plains." Sully smirked. "Time to go earn that good money of yours."

Lou felt his heart sink down to his stomach.

8

THE OUTPOST

LOU GOT another shock soon after.

Not only were they headed out onto the plains, out into the darkness, but they were going to take horses with them.

Lou felt a mixture of feelings about that. He was happy to have something beneath him that could do the running if he needed it, but, at the same time, he was anxious that he might just as easily slip off its back and break his neck. And what if some of those cursed wolves Sully had been talking about decided to rip the horse's throat out?

Although Rut's calming words had gone some way to reassuring him, to stopping him taking *everything* Sully said at face value, he admitted to himself that he was still reasonably wary about the whole thing.

He'd spent his whole life being scared of the dark, of venturing out onto the plains at night, and he still hadn't seen anything close up likely to change that opinion in a hurry.

Sully brought them to the stables beneath the fort that Lou had never known existed. There were five horses all there, swaying on their feet as they slept. They were all black as the night and he caught whiff of that horsey smell of theirs, that scent so strong that it make the back of his throat tang.

Sully approached the first horse, removed his glove, then reached out and gently stroked its mane. It snorted and shook its big head, sending its mane dancing about, shimmering in the light from the torches. Sally stroked its nose, soothing it from its sleep, then he glanced back over his shoulder at Lou, then smiled slightly. "Come on. They don't bite."

Lou wasn't so sure. He remembered being a kid, when he'd been playing out in the square one day. A cart had come rolling into town, its cartwheels bucking against the cobblestones, and before he'd known it, those clopping hooves had drowned out all sound, and he had found himself beneath a pair of *huge* carthorses.

The driver had pulled them up, stopped them right there. But Lou had tumbled to the ground out of shock, and he still remembered that numbing feeling that'd crawled up from the base of his spine as he'd landed on his bottom on the hard cobblestones.

That night his ma had found out from one of the neighbours and sent him to his room for putting himself in such danger. He wondered how she might feel now, knowing that he was out here, playing at being a skuller.

All the same, Lou got another reassuring glance off Sully and approached the second horse along. Just like the first horse, it was sleeping. And so Lou copied exactly what he'd seen Sully do.

He reached up and stroked its mane, feeling the rugged hair against his fingertips, and he felt its nerves contract as it came around. He took a step back and he felt the horse jab its head in his direction.

He took another step back, feeling that familiar childhood fear coming back to him now, biting him hot and hard. He bumped up against the rickety wooden fence behind him, making it creak and groan, and he clung onto it as if he was on a ship caught in a storm, and he was steadying himself.

The horse shook its head a couple of times, snorted, then clopped its hooves. Next it turned away from him and apparently went back off to sleep.

Sully rounded his own horse and said, "You've gotta be gentle and firm with them, otherwise they won't respect you. They know what kinda danger we're going out there to face, so they've gotta know their rider knows just what he's doin'. Else they're not gonna let you so much as feed them a carrot."

Lou still felt his heart pounding against his ribcage, that fear stabbing him in the gut. He felt more scared now than he had out on the plains. The smells of the horses got stronger and sharper and he felt like he might be sick.

Sully approached Lou's horse and went through that same routine of his. The stroking the nose, the weaving his bare fingers in and out of the mane, and, just like the first, the horse came round from sleep, opened up its eyes and looked ready for work.

Sully glanced back at Lou, a faint smile tracing his lips. "This ain't gonna be too tricky for you this time. He's gonna see his buddy going out to work and he's just gonna follow his flanks. Be a different matter altogether when you're doin' this on your own, though. When you get to that point you're gonna have to get over that fear of yours. If you ever wanna be a *real* skuller, that is."

Lou looked to the horse again, to those matted black eyes, just the hint of light in them. All his life he'd learned to fear beasts, animals. Even the ones they kept for meat in the safe confines of the village. And he guessed that he'd have to work hard to get over his fear.

As Sully's words sank in, though, he found himself getting even more swept away not by the prospect that he might have to do this horse-waking thing on his own at some point, although that did mightily scare him, but that he would be going out onto his own into the plains.

And then he thought of the money.

The grung he could make.

The winters that he could feed his family for.

If he only stuck to being a skuller a few years he might save up enough to buy his own farm, or maybe Rut would be interested in going in together on one. He seemed a good-hearted man. Maybe they could go in together with Sully too.

Perhaps when they got back from checking out the outpost Lou could float the idea.

If they got back from the outpost at all, that was.

Sully kept the pace of his horse gentle. And he kept on looking back over his shoulder. It seemed that Rut was telling the truth when he'd said Sully would take good care of him. He seemed concerned about him, anyway. Lou wondered if it was just because Sully would get in trouble if he got a green skuller killed on his first night out on the plains.

There were several dozen torches all laid out across the plains. They were placed around a hundred or so yards apart, just leaving enough darkness between them to ignite Lou's imagination.

They followed the glare of the torches, Lou clinging on tight to the reins, squeezing his knees into his horse's flanks, listening to its panting as it kept up with Sully's horse.

The smell of sweaty horse flesh was almost overpowering, smothering his mouth and nose as he felt his body jerk from side to side as he sat in the saddle.

His mouth was dry, parched even, but he was too afraid of falling off to make a grab for the water canister which hung down by his thigh. He needed both his hands for the reins.

Sully upped the pace a little as they plunged deeper and deeper into the plains. So much so that Lou could feel the chill of the night wind bustling all round the collar of his tunic. He felt himself shudder, his teeth chatter, in that mixture of fear and cold.

They'd been riding for about an hour, or so Lou imagined, when Sully slowed down to a walk, with Lou's horse just copying automatically.

Five torches, all stumped into the ground, stood in a pentagram, all around what Lou recognised as the central outpost from his morning rides to Old Man Junth's farm.

In the morning light it was a ramshackle, but towering, construction, several improvised floors of wood, about ten storeys high, hastily put together by inexpert craftsmen, most likely the skullers themselves, and Lou had always thought of it looking wildly out of place out here in the middle of the plains.

As he followed Sully riding his horse about the perimeter of the outpost, Lou noticed how Sully now held his crossbow in one hand, and his head frequently jerked from point to point as he caught some motion or other. Lou thought about placing his hand on the hilt of his sword, or even bringing out his own crossbow, but he couldn't seem to shift his fingers from their locked position on the reins.

Sully walked his horse inside the torches standing outside the outpost, his eyes still quick and smooth as they moved about the façade.

If Lou had had any sort of control whatsoever over his horse he might've just hung back, outside the torches, to let Sully get on with whatever it was that he was looking for. But as his horse simply followed Sully's, it seemed that he had no choice in the matter. And then Sully did something that just totally caught Lou sideways, like a fist to the temple.

Sully brought his horse to a stop and then hurled himself to the ground.

Of course, when Sully's horse stopped, so did Lou's. He had no choice in the matter. And, with a swift look round his surroundings, and realising that he could make out little beyond the glow of the torches, he decided he'd be better off getting down from his horse too.

And so, somehow managing not to land on his head, Lou dismounted, and immediately unsheathed his sword, for some reason thinking that it made tactical sense to have one of them bearing a crossbow, a long-range weapon, while the other had a sword, much more proficient at short-range.

Sully tied up both horses to the earthed wooden pole which stood at the entrance to the outpost, then he glanced back over his shoulder and gave Lou a grim smile. "You be careful with that sword of yours, yeah? Could do with not getting any limbs slashed off in the middle of the plains."

Lou let loose a nervous chuckle, but his chattering teeth soon took care of that. And he followed Sully into the outpost, into the thick darkness of the interior.

Inside, Lou was immediately struck with that all-too-familiar stench of blood. That smell reminded him of rust, like farm tools that got left out in the rain. It was an unnatural smell, and it turned his stomach even to think about it.

Sully sparked a flame out of somewhere, and lit up a torch which he held out over the interior of the outpost.

There, lying all about the floor, there were corpses.

Skullers, every last one of them.

All dressed in their all-black uniforms, black as the night.

Lou felt a scream die in his throat, and his logical mind somehow kicked in, as if trying to smother out the emotional side, to keep his sanity about him. He counted the bodies.

Seven.

Seven of them.

Then he took in the details.

The throats all ravaged. Crimson blood glistening in the torch-light. He felt heat rise up inside him, and before he knew it, it was too late, and he doubled over, retching.

When Lou recovered, shivering all the more, he saw Sully peering close to one of the corpses. He slipped Lou a sidelong glance, then said, "Wolves."

Lou felt his teeth chattering and his skin become plagued with goose bumps. "How . . . how can you be sure?"

With his free hand, Sully pointed with his finger to one of the skuller's wounds. "You can tell by the bite mark. Not big enough to be a bear, that's for sure." He straightened up again and met Lou's eye. "Nah, definitely wolves."

Lou glanced about him, to those corpses. All of them wore the same expression, that gaping wide mouth, the eyes peeled back to show almost all their whites, and all of them with weapons clasped in their hands.

Maces. Crossbows. Swords.

And their muscles still taut as cables as they clung on.

Lou wanted to get out. He wanted to get back on the horse and ride back to Endmere. But, at the same time, he knew that he couldn't go. Not till Sully said so. He had to keep himself together. He had to make a success of himself as a skuller.

Otherwise his family would suffer.

Sully curtailed his inspection of the corpses and unsheathed his own sword. He held it down at his thigh, and stalked deeper into the outpost, holding the torch out before him to light the way. He glanced back to Lou, and urged him forward.

Lou was so numb with fear and revolt, that he felt his legs moving beneath him, following Sully on his way up through the tower, up those improvised steps that twirled upwards, listening to the battered and weathered wooden planks groan beneath his feet, and trying to get shot of that moist taste and stench of blood from his mouth. He gripped the hilt of his sword tighter, feeling the tough material there, feeling it rub against his calloused hands.

About halfway up the stairs, he heard a muffled, but distinct groan.

And the gnashing of teeth.

9

WOLF

LOU'S HEART dropped right down to his stomach, and he felt all those smells, those sights, the bodies, all overwhelm him for a moment. And he stood stunned, almost rendered unable to understand Sully's husky whisper, for him to attack with him.

Lou just watched on, beleaguered, as Sully grasped hold of his sword, raised it over his head and, still holding the torch down by his side, rushed into the room.

Lou stood out on the stairs as he listened to the crunch of bone against blade, the slicing of skin, and a few more groans.

And then there was silence.

All sound stopped.

Lou could only hear his own heartbeat thumping away in his eardrums. And then everything rushed right back to him like a torrent of spring water.

He took hold of his own sword, squeezing that ragged material tight, and he rushed into the room, after Sully. And he took it all in, stretched out before him.

Sully slouched slightly, with the tip of his sword resting against the uneven floor of the outpost. His shoulders rose and fell with his breathing, still recovering from the exertion.

The torch lay on the ground, to one side, still flickering away, and the edge of Sully's sword was bloody. And only then did it occur to Lou to look down at where Sully stared.

There, on the floor, was a cursed wolf, its flanks opened, its ribs showing, several of them cracked now, and its organs spilling out in a bloody garnish. Beneath the wolf lay a skuller, flinching now and again, one eye open as he looked them over.

Sully snapped back to look at Lou, jerked his head in the direction of the skuller and the wolf. And Lou realised what he wanted him to do.

Lou sheathed his sword once again, then padded over the wooden floor, listening to the planks creak beneath him. He stared for a few seconds at the cursed wolf, clearly dead now, its tongue lolling out from between its jaws, and its bright red eyes that all cursed animals had, apparently dead. Even so, he had to look back to Sully one more time, just to check he wasn't about to get himself bitten.

Sully just gave him a nod, his chest still heaving and sweat running down his cheeks.

Lou crunched his teeth together, determined now that he wasn't going to be a coward any longer, and he felt for the furry frame of the cursed wolf.

Its fur was still warm when he touched it, and matted with the still-breathing skuller's blood. He closed his eyes as he prised the wolf off the skuller's body and then tipped it to one side.

Its corpse landed with a muted *thud*, and then Lou turned his attention to the skuller.

The skuller had a bite mark on his neck, a little above his shoulder blade, just to the side of his throat. If the wolf had got him a hair's breadth to the other side then he would've been just like his friends downstairs.

A corpse.

But he was still breathing, just. Although Lou noted that each breath he took seemed to be shallower than the last. The skuller could hardly find the strength to speak now. The blood drenched the front of his tunic, and Lou saw that he continued to clutch his sword in his fist, his knuckles white from the strength of his grip, and he realised that the skuller had at least been making some job of fighting back against the wolf before they'd arrived.

Sully arrived at Lou's shoulder, so the two of them now stood close to the dying skuller, able to hear his croaky, cracked voice. When the skuller spoke, Lou could hear the bloody spittle frothing at the back of his throat. "... *She*," he said. "*She*."

Lou looked to Sully, expecting him to explain what he meant by this, but Sully looked just as vacant as he did. He turned back to the skuller to see what else he had to say.

The skuller's eyes rolled back in their sockets, and he seemed to lose himself to the fever of his pain for several seconds, before he could meet their gaze again. He sucked hard, but it was clear that he could hardly take in any air at all. "She," he said, again.

"Who's 'she?'" Sully said, the muscles in his face drawing tight.

The skuller blinked a couple of times, then looked down to his sword, to the thin layer of the cursed wolf's blood smeared on it. He looked a little surprised, as if he'd totally forgotten what he was doing there, what that sword was doing in his hand, and then he turned back to the two of them. ". . . She . . . she . . . she."

Sully glanced to Lou and shrugged, then he reached for the canister he kept down at his thigh. He uncorked it then held it to the dying skuller's lips. As the canister touched his lips, the skuller's eyes widened and he drank deeply from it. He closed his lips tight when he'd had enough, sending a little of the water running down his chin and onto his bloodied tunic.

The skuller sank back against the wall, now barely able to keep his eyes open. His hand flexed on the hilt of his sword a few times, and for a moment it looked like he might let it go.

But he held on.

He held onto it until his dying breath.

As Sully and Lou crouched over the skuller, he let loose his final, husky, dying breath. And then he was still. His eyes staring out into the space before him, fixed just above the carcass of the cursed wolf.

Sully turned back to Lou, his lips slightly parted, but eyes just as jaded as might be expected from seeing dead skullers on a regular basis, and then he got himself up from the floor.

He withdrew a rag from within the pocket of his trousers and wiped the blood from his blade. Without turning round, he said, "I'm going to check the rest of the outpost. Wait with the horses, won't you?"

Lou didn't argue with Sully, as afraid as he was of going back down, of passing those corpses for a second time. He knew that he had to get braver. That he had to get accustomed to this . . . to this *death*.

He picked his way through the bodies, doing his best not to meet any of those dead gazes, and then he got himself outside, back out onto the plains. He looked to the horses, still tied up, and then looked off into the darkness.

Right on the horizon, he could see the sky turning a shade of light blue.

Soon it would be dawn, and then the sun would rise. And the cursed animals would be gone. He wondered what time it might be, and he thought that, if this was a normal day, if he'd still been tending to the fields, he might be getting up at this time, getting himself ready to take the cart out to Old Man Junth's.

But now things were different.

He was a skuller.

Now he lived in a different time.

Whereas before he'd been dedicated to the space between the dawn and the dusk, and free from danger, now he found himself occupying that deadly area between dusk and dawn.

And if he wanted to stay alive he needed to keep his wits about him.

Sully came back out of the outpost about ten minutes later. He carried the torch with him, then dropped it on the ground and allowed the dew-covered grass to extinguish it. He brushed past Lou, and headed to his horse.

Lou felt rooted to the spot, his blood tingling through his veins, almost unable to take anything else in, still absorbing the shock of the mounted dead bodies.

And that stench of blood.

He knew that from now on all his nightmares would be

stashed full of that smell, and that sight. He listened to the gentle *creak* of Sully loosening the rope which tied up his horse to the wooden post. "What about the bodies?" Lou found himself saying.

Sully hauled himself up onto the back of his horse, then looked to him. "We'll send someone to pick them up later on, when it's daylight. We'll need some more men to get them all packed up. More than the two of us can handle."

"What do you think he meant by 'she?'"

Sully smirked slightly, and then his expression straightened out, as if he was only then realising the full implications of the question. "I don't know. Dying men say all manner of things. He was probably delirious." His expression got even more grave. "After fighting off that cursed wolf, seeing and hearing all his brothers-in-arms die for so long, that can only drive a man crazy."

Lou swallowed, then headed over to his own horse. He was acutely aware of Sully gazing at him as he stuck his foot into the stirrup, then hoisted himself up, at second time of trying, onto the back of the horse. He found the indentation of the saddle much quicker this time, and felt just a fraction more comfortable.

Sully gave him a half-smile. "You're looking more and more at home on that thing. I would take care, else we might make a skuller of you yet."

After all they'd seen that night, riding out into this previously unknown and hugely dangerous domain, Lou felt strangely close to Sully. It was like the two of them were survivors, like they'd skirted the Land of the Dead, and managed to come back from it alive. He wondered if Sully felt the same way, or if so many brushes with death and dying men had inoculated him.

And yet, Lou felt safe enough in Sully's company to ask the question.

"I . . . I don't know if I can do this," Lou said. "It's just, I don't think I'm brave enough." He paused, again to swallow away a lump in his throat. "Back there, on the stairs, I was afraid. I couldn't move from the spot. And then . . . and then, it was too late."

Sully surveyed him, gave him a once over, and then cracked his reins down on the back of his horse, leading them off back across the plains, back towards Endmere. "Don't you think that's how we all started out?" He rode on, and Lou kicked his own horse into action, going after him. "This wasn't anything big, no big problem. Just a solitary cursed wolf. Let's just hope that next time it happens, next time we run into something like this you're ready to leap into action." He glanced back over his shoulder. "Because when we run into a pack of cursed wolves or, worse, a pack of cursed *bears*, then it'll take at least the two of us to have any chance of getting out alive."

They rode on, heading between the flaming torches. And with each *clop* of hoof, Lou felt them getting closer to Endmere, drawing nearer to safety. Soon he would be able to say that he had survived a night out on the plains, returned to tell the tale, and if he could just get grip on his fear then he knew he could make it as a skuller.

And yet, that episode, where he'd been standing on the stairwell, listening to Sully fighting against the cursed wolf, doing his best to save that other skuller's life. If Lou had gone with him might he have been in time to save the skuller from his mortal wounds?

As he felt the muscles of the horse ripple against the sides of his legs, he swore that, when the next time rolled round, he wouldn't act the coward. He would get over it. However hard it was. He had a sword, after all, and these animals just had claws and teeth.

He had the advantage.

As they climbed the hill at the edge of the plains, and reached the summit, Lou viewed the steady glow of light up ahead of them. And he thought of the sun, rising up, dawning on the new day. Then, in a flash of realisation, he recalled that the sun rose behind them, that in front of them, behind Endmere, it set.

As he reached the cusp of the hill, drew up alongside where Sully had stopped, he saw that Endmere was on fire. That flames the height of towers flickered up above the village.

And then the screams carried on the morning breeze.

Lou felt a boiling anger seize hold of his gut.

10

ENDMERE ABLAZE

S ULLY CLACKED his heels, and clicked his tongue, and his horse jostled off down the hill.

Lou just stood there, feeling his fury grow inside him as he watched his hometown, all he'd ever known of comfort and safety, slowly crackling into ash.

Thick black smoke coiled up into the morning sky, dirtying the otherwise cloudless day. He snapped to his senses and kicked his own horse on down the slope, after Sully.

As they got closer, within about fifty yards, Lou felt the heat up against his cheek, the burning warmth there. They drew nearer still and found themselves covered in a billowing cloud of ash.

Lou brought the neck of his tunic up to cover his mouth and nose, and closed his eyes, feeling them tear up in the relentless heat. For some reason he thought of his ma's kitchen, her cooking there, burning some bread or something else.

He caught ash in his mouth, on his tongue, and he felt his mind get caught in a spin.

Next thing he knew he was tumbling through the air, tossed off the back of his horse. He listened to the hooves pounding against the earth as it fled the smoke, not willing to go with its rider into the inferno.

Lou's heart pulsed in his mouth, and his tongue tasted thick with blood. His back tingled from where he'd fallen, and a blinding pain struck his leg.

He could hear shouting and screaming nearby, cutting through the crackle of the flames and the crumbling of the wooden structures.

He forced himself up to his feet, and barrelled forward, heading into the heat of the fire, determined that he wouldn't be afraid.

Not now.

The smoke got even thicker. He held his tunic right up to his eyes, only allowing himself a narrow slit to look out from. He could just about make out the forms of the buildings through the thick smoke. It was impossible to tell where the fire was coming from, just that it had seemingly spread everywhere, ignited everything in its path.

Lou reached out and touched a brick wall. He felt the bricks all warmed up there, beneath his touch, and he used it to guide him.

Up ahead he saw a break in the smoke, and he headed for it. Seconds later he realised that it was the town square. The eye of the firestorm. He stumbled over the cobblestones, feeling the warmth coming up through the soles of his boots.

He saw several bundled figures in the spot, in the middle here. He trudged up to them, his leg still biting with pain. He looked them over, a dozen or so of them, all their faces painted black with ash, their features obscured.

Unreadable.

And then he saw her.

His sis.

Syre.

She sat at the edge of the group, her clothes and exposed skin just as black with ash as the rest of them, her knees tucked up to her chest.

Lou lurched forward, suddenly feeling drunk with all the smoke layering his lungs. He picked his way through the others, checking out their faces. He saw a couple of his neighbours, people he recognised.

But they didn't seem to see him.

They just stared on ahead, as if hypnotised by the rising smoke. And he knew they'd given up. That they could see no way out of here, no way to escape Endmere. Right now, though, they were the least of Lou's concern, and he strode up to Syre, crouched down, and then embraced her.

Slowly, he felt her take hold of him in her grip. She squeezed him tight, and then, as Lou rose up from the ground, he took her with him, got her back onto her feet. He stared into her blackened face, feeling his chest almost splitting in two. "Ma? Pa?" Lou said.

His sis just stared ahead of her into the smoke. That look that Lou was now beginning to associate with death, with everyone who brushed close to death. And he had no need to prompt her for another answer. She clutched a book to her chest. It was leather-bound, its yellowed pages splayed and sticking out the edges.

He glanced about the others, their neighbours. He had to

shout to make himself heard. "Come on!" he said. "We've gotta get out of here!"

One or two of them offered a glance in his direction. Through the soot he recognised Poels, the working hand that he'd asked for money, and who'd given him enough for some brandy wine. But he didn't seem to see Lou. He just stared off into that rising smoke.

Apparently lost in the blackness.

Lou tried to rouse the others, with Syre clinging to his tunic, but they were all apparently lost to the smoke too, not at all interested in getting up. He shouted out to them till he felt his lungs ache from the effort, and then, behind him, he heard a gigantic *snap* of wood, followed by a *thunk* and a scattering of sparks.

They had to get out.

They had to get out now.

Before the whole damn place burned down.

He noticed that the breaking of the wood had cut off the way he'd got into Endmere. He would have to find another way out for them. He looked off across the square, and picked out *The Mocker's Pit*.

It smouldered away, like the rest of the buildings.

Then he recalled the basement, the one where they took the deliveries of brandy wine and ginger ale. The basement tunnel led to just outside the town, so that the heavier-laden carts didn't have to come inside. That might be their way out.

If the tunnel hadn't collapsed in the fire.

Again, he looked to those ashen faces, even reached out and shook the neighbours. But no one would acknowledge him. Not even Poels. They just stared into the ever-rising smoke.

Reluctantly, Lou left them behind, feeling Syre cling tight to his tunic, take the material tight in her fists. It reminded him of when she'd been a baby, and she'd clung to his fingers hard like that. He had to save her now. He was all she had left.

She was all *he* had left.

He tried to loosen the book from her hands, but had no success. She gripped it as tight as she held his hand.

They ran on.

Smoke jetted out through the smashed-in windows of *The Mocker's Pit*, and Lou kept Syre close him. He watched the smoke and saw how it rose. If they could just keep to the floor, go in there on hands and knees, he was sure they'd be able to find their way through.

He jerked Syre down beside him, and the two of them crawled their way in through the doorway to *The Mocker's*, keeping their heads below the smoke.

Even without the smoke blowing right in his face, Lou could hardly breathe. He was relying on the few times he'd come in here before. When he'd been running some piece of his pa's work to show to the landlord, Simvun, a man with a large, ginger beard which lay against the curve of his belly.

There was no sign of the landlord now though, as they made their way through the place, hugging the turn of the bar, picking their way over the fallen lumber, and burning fires.

They turned the corner into the bar. And then, a few paces ahead, Lou saw the trapdoor.

It sat there, snug, flush with the floor.

And he tugged Syre before him, and pushed her onwards towards it.

Lou tugged at the iron loop which acted as a handle several times before he could get it to budge as much as an inch. Finally, he managed to open it a crack and keep it open by fitting his fist into the gap.

He called Syre out from her daze and had her help him tug the trapdoor open.

It creaked back on its hinge, giving off the smoky depths down below, and the all-encompassing gloom. Then, after first shoving himself down inside, then taking Syre with him, they made their way through the tunnel, following the gently rising slope that led to the outside of Endmere.

And to the perils of the plains.

By the time the sun set that evening, the skullers had taken charge.

Lou, along with the others, had managed to set up a series of tents, and to create a perimeter around the camp. They'd discussed it between them all, wondered whether it might be better to beat a retreat for the nearest village over, but had decided it too dangerous to risk getting caught out on the plains.

It was better that they stay in one place, at least for tonight.

Whenever Lou had a loose moment, he spent his time looking after Syre, cuddling her to his chest, telling her it was going to be all right. He got little out of her. She hadn't said a word to him since he'd found her in the square, and he just guessed he had to leave her to her own devices to let her get over it.

Lou watched the last of the smoke rising from Endmere, and he looked out over all the buildings, their shops, their houses—their *homes*—that they'd never again have. They'd lost everything.

Absolutely everything.

And, just as Lou found himself thinking of his ma and pa, he turned his thoughts to his savings, the little of his wages he'd got on that last day of working for Old Man Junth. Those had gone too.

Gone up in smoke just like the rest of it.

As the sun went down behind the trees in a cascade of tangerine-oranges, and hazy-purples, Lou smelled the roasting sausages being cooked up on the campfires, listened to the crackle of the flames, and he knew he'd never think the same way about that sound again.

Forever more, for him, fire would be synonymous with destruction and pain and loss.

He tucked his sis into her bed, plumped up her pillow and made sure she was as comfy as could be with a half-charred scrap of wool they'd salvaged from the burning village as a blanket. She still held onto that book, and he had no chance at prising it away from her.

Giving up, he headed outside to the campfire, where the skullers kept watch.

Lou looked to Murch, then to Rut, finally to Sully. All of them hunched about the fire there. They were the only survivors. The rest of the skullers had been killed in the fire, either half-asleep as the flames had licked at their toes while they slept in their bunks, or killed as they tried to raise the alarm, to get people out. No one had anything to say. And Lou couldn't think of anything either. It was Murch who finally broke the silence.

Murch shook his head, long and drawn out, the shining skin of his scar catching the firelight. "Never seen a fire spread that fast in all my life. There just weren't no time to get people out. To raise the alarm."

Rut, with his puffed up cheeks, slipped Murch a sidelong

glance, then turned his attention back to the rippling flames of the campfire before them.

Lou straightened his back then looked Murch in the eye. "What d'you think started it?"

Again, Murch shook his head. "Not a clue."

"Doesn't really matter, does it?" Rut said. "It's happened now. Gotta think about how we're gonna handle this."

Lou felt his heart well in his throat. "Do we go back in there tomorrow, when it's light? See if we can find something"—his voice cracked—"*bury* our dead?"

A long silence fell over them, then Murch scratched the back of his neck. "Best thing by my reckoning is getting these people to safety first. Don't wanna get caught by the night again. Staying out on the plains tonight is bad enough."

Lou felt a throb of anger take hold of him. "But this is everything they've got. We have to do *something* for them. Surely there are some things we can salvage."

Lou at least expected to be told off by Murch, to be put in his place as the rookie skuller, and yet there was no reply from him, or anyone.

That was until Sully stirred from where he sat, and looked to Lou. "Think what's maybe gone over your head is that there's no doubt to our minds what caused this fire."

"And what's that?" Lou said.

"Witchcraft."

11

VILLAGES OF ASHES

NOT MUCH transpired in the course of the night. At least, Lou was glad that no packs of cursed wolves, or bears, for that matter, cropped up to cause them grief. Although he had half-expected it.

As he sat there, slumped up against a burned piece of timber with his sword fixed in his fist, he'd thought long and hard about the wolves or bears coming and wondered whether he'd have had the strength to even fight. Even looking to his fellow skullers, to Rut, Murch and Sully, he saw that they were weary, that they'd lost several friends in the fire, not to mention most everyone they knew.

Lou felt the chill of the dawn on his cheeks, and the dew creeping up the leg of his trousers, making the material damp. He zoned in on every sound. Every so often there was a *creak* followed by a *thud* as more wood fell back at Endmere, as the fire beat itself into a steady, cool death.

He breathed in that wood smoke on the breeze, and wondered if he could smell human flesh there too.

And just the thought of it turned his stomach yet again.

Like all the others, he mutely went about collecting up the camp, folding the tarpaulins, and getting ready to move out. They had rounded up six horses from the village, including the two he and Sully had ridden to the outpost. The survivors numbered about thirty. Everyone had lost several family members in the fire, not to mention all their possessions. All anyone had now was the ashen clothes on their backs. And, thinking about it, Lou thought that the only clothes he had anymore was the skuller's uniform he wore.

Murch took charge of the party, leading them across the plains, between the now burned-out torches. No one had been to light them the night before. There simply hadn't been the manpower to do so. And it might be that they'd never be lit again. Endmere was gone so there was no need for them to keep the darkness back at night any longer.

As they reached the summit of the hill which overlooked Endmere, Lou risked a final glance back over his shoulder. It was a sorry sight. Just a pit of ashes, still smoking away ever so lightly. He thought he could make out the last remnants of *The Mocker's Pit*, but who was to know for sure? He would say that much for fire— that it was a great leveller, it sent everything back to its element.

He led the horse with the reins, and looked up to Syre sitting there, on the saddle, holding tightly. Her face was sallow, her eyes almost struck with jaundice, and her skin was forever stained with ash. She didn't look back over her shoulder. She just kept staring forwards. Still completely and totally transfixed. And she still had that book clutched to her chest. He tried to read the title but had no luck. It was obscured by her fingers. It looked like one of his ma's old books. She was probably just holding onto it out of shock.

An hour or so later they reached the next village along, Quagsmile. And Lou felt a familiar lurch in his chest as he saw that, just like Endmere, it'd been reduced to a pile of smoking ashes.

Lou watched as Rut rushed away from their party, rampaging down the valley and towards the town of Quagsmile. He remembered him saying that it was his home town. And the same fate had befallen it. As he peeled back his gaze, checked back on Syre to see if she'd been affected, he caught Sully's eye.

Sully looked to have a new emptiness to his gaze. And he kept his hand hovering over the hilt of his sword, as if they might be on the point of being jumped by cursed animals at any second. His shoulders were rigid, and his cheeks pitted.

Lou found himself struck dumb by the intensity of his appearance.

And then, just like that, Sully gazed back down into the valley. Like the rest of the group staring off after Rut, who was crying out into the early morning sun, screaming out the names of people who could only be his family. Lou felt his heart wrench and he squeezed the reins in his fist.

Then he followed Murch's lead as they proceeded on down into the valley, and to the village below.

They picked through the rubble of Quagsmile for hours. They turned up some stores of food, extra clothing that might come in handy later on. But they found no survivors. When Lou accompanied Sully and Murch to check out the skullers' fortification, they only found dead bodies there.

It appeared that they'd all died in their beds.

Murch shook his head as he stepped back from the dormitory, where they'd found all the bodies of the skullers. "Looks to me like the fire started here before sundown. Caught everyone unawares. Wasn't like back at Endmere where it cropped up in the middle of the night, when at least the skullers had the chance to warn everyone."

Lou stared at those charred faces, their clothing melted into their burned-up skin. He thought about how easily it might've been him, if he hadn't ventured out with Sully to the outpost. And even there they'd seen death, the skullers ripped apart by cursed wolves. It seemed like whichever way he ran, Lou would come face to face with death.

It was around midday before Murch thought to call a meeting, to have everyone brought in together to discuss just what they were going to do next. When Murch spoke he chewed on his tongue, apparently stressed at the situation they found themselves in.

Lou just kept himself to the fringe of the group, keeping close to Syre, as if she might slip away from him too if he wasn't paying attention.

Murch cleared his throat, and fished out a wooden crate, smothered in ash but still for the most part sturdy looking.

Lou counted thirty-four survivors in all, collected around Murch. Only thirty-odd survivors from two towns which between them had once numbered in the hundreds. He caught a strong whiff of the ash carrying on the wind, and he felt it dry his throat.

He squeezed Syre closer to his chest, feeling all her muscles still stiff.

"We have a decision to make," Murch said, his squat, throaty voice carrying much further than Lou would've thought. "Way I see it, we've got two choices, here." He looked over the group, his small eyes peeping through those chubby cheeks of his. "Could go on along the road, beat the track till we reach the next village over, Gwindermere. But, the way things are going, along with the silence of the traffic along the road, makes me think that we might just end up coming up against the same thing."

He peered over the crowd, catching Lou's eye for a second, before moving on to someone else. "The other thing we could do is head along Capital Road, head up on it to Ilsnare. The Crystal City."

That description, 'The Crystal City,' had always resonated with Lou. He'd often pictured hundreds of glass buildings, all of them gleaming in the sun. And he admitted to himself that he was excited about seeing what it might be really like.

Someone on the front row called out.

A woman in her forties or fifties, with tangled blond pigtails dangling down over her front. "Aintcha heard?" she said. "Ilsnare's cursed. That'll be the last place for us to go."

Lou thought this over. Of course he knew that Ilsnare was cursed, it had been cursed ever since he could remember, before he was ever born. That was where the cursed animals came from.

Some people spoke about a magical mist which lingered over the whole place in the evenings, and the early morning. It turned the wine to vinegar, and the water to grease. And the animals, of course. The ones it didn't turn baron, got cursed and wandered out here, into the countryside.

That was why they needed skullers.

Lots of people chatted about the explanation for the curse, where it had come from. But Lou knew that no one really knew where it came from. That did nothing to calm his fear, though. In fact, he was terrified.

Murch considered the woman, then said, "Yeah, well, we ain't exactly got much choice, do we? All's I know is it'd be better for us not to spend another night out here on the plains. We'll get ourselves torn apart sooner or later, that's for certain."

"That's better than livin' in a cursed place," the woman replied.

There was a lot of mumbling among the assembled crowd, the survivors from Endmere.

It seemed like the group was totally split down the middle. Lou himself had no idea which way they should turn. He couldn't help feeling that if they carried on, if they just kept on their way to the next village then perhaps they'd find it well, everything as normal.

Then they could start their re-building.

As much as he wanted to see The Crystal City some day, he knew that his priority was to keep Syre safe, and she'd be much safer out here, in the countryside, where everything was at least familiar.

"Guess we'll take us a vote, then, huh?" Murch said, rubbing his perspiring forehead.

It was a simple choice, just like Murch said, and the results came in quickly. While a third of the survivors voted on heading to Ilsnare, the other two thirds voted for them to carry along the road, to get to the next village.

Murch shook his head from side to side, but climbed down from his charred wooden crate, accepting the decision. Still shaking his head, he made his way through the crowd, then brushed by Lou, who heard him mutter to him, under his breath, "We're for it now. We make it to Gwindermere and it's in the same way, we're gonna be out here on the plains for the night. No two ways about it."

Lou watched Murch head off to make the preparations for them to move out.

It took them another few hours to reach Gwindermere, and when they did, just as soon as Lou saw the town peeking up over the hill beside them, he knew that the same thing had happened.

They went through the same routine, their ragged survivors checking through the place for anyone that might still be alive amongst the burned-out buildings. But, just like Quagsmile, there was no one at all.

Lou looked to Rut, who hadn't said a word on the whole trip. He wanted to reassure him somehow, tell him that, just like him, he'd lost his ma and pa in a fire.

But the way that Rut looked, the way his cheekbones looked firm and solid, as he was grinding his teeth, Lou thought it best just to leave him to his own deliberations.

Murch didn't gloat at all about having been right. About having warned them to go to Ilsnare. He simply went about gathering up the camp, issuing orders to the survivors, and getting them into place. He had them build the camp in a horseshoe shape, which Lou reasoned to himself meant the skullers could better look over the place as the dusk rolled in, and the animals cropped up on the plains.

Whatever else Lou thought of Murch, he had to admit that he knew how to lead people, knew how to keep people safe.

Or perhaps he just knew how to look active about it.

They prepared for their second night out on the plains, and Lou felt himself shuddering a little. Partially it was because of the brisk autumn wind bustling down the hillside, and also because of the prospect of being called into action. Of having to defend these people from the cursed animals. Now was no time for cowardice. Now he had to protect Syre. If anything happened to her then he would never forgive himself.

And so he got Syre all set up with her canvas tent. He tucked her into bed with a thick lambs-wool blanket they'd salvaged from Quagsmile earlier on, and he lit a candle at the entrance to the tent, so that she wouldn't be cast into total darkness as she slept. He would want to check on her throughout the night. Again, that book was still in her arms. She wouldn't let go of it.

Outside, just like the night before, Sully set a fire in the middle of the tents, so that there was a warmth glow passing over the whole of the campsite. Then, Lou helping him, they proceeded to light up the torches and place them round the camp, so they'd have a fair chance at spotting any cursed animals that might try creeping up on them.

Lou watched on as Murch barked orders at the survivors, as the sun set over the hillside, and the dusk rolled in. Murch made sure everyone was back inside their tent, out of harm's way, so that the skullers could do their job.

Soon enough, only Murch, Rut, Sully and Lou remained outside in the biting night air.

Up above him, Lou could see the stars cascading up in the

heavens. It was a clear night. What they'd often used to call, a *fair* night.

No smell of rain in the air.

Not even the hint of a cloud on the horizon.

In the middle distance an owl was hooting away. And everything seemed so still to Lou. The wind had even dropped from earlier, but that hadn't made things any warmer, although the fire in the middle of the tents, and the torches at the periphery of their campsite did help a little.

Murch set them in pairs, Lou with Sully, and himself with Rut, and he ordered Lou and Sully to take the first watch over the campsite. He instructed them to wake him around midnight, for them to take up their shift.

The way they'd work it was that if Lou or Sully ran into any trouble, saw anything they couldn't handle between the two of them, then they were to wake Murch and Rut.

Lou felt a quiet confidence flow through him as he thought of himself being alongside Sully. That made him feel a whole lot better.

Just a smidge braver.

Sully took charge, of course, sending Lou to go and patrol the other side of the campsite, for him to stalk through the gloom, and to keep his crossbow ready to fly at a second's notice. He told him that it might be the difference between life and death. And not just for Lou, but for all the survivors.

With that in mind, Lou chewed on his tongue, trying to drive himself more awake, to get himself prepared to take on anything.

12

A CLOAKED FIGURE

ON THE OTHER SIDE of the tents, things got pretty lonely. After several hours that owl hooting in the distance seemed like a ghoul to Lou, and every time the owl hooted he felt a slight tingle scuttle up his spine.

The Moon shone down on him, sending that cool, gleaming light all around, over the plains, setting them in a light that was impossible to trust. He knew that he could only trust the light coming from the torches.

He gripped his crossbow tight, feeling the narrow weave of its grip slip into the callouses on his hands. He breathed in the oily scent of it, the greased up mechanism, and, realising that he hadn't drunk anything all day, he reached for his canister and wet his mouth with ash-flavoured water.

As he replaced the canister, he knew something was wrong. Whether it was the *crunch* of a branch being trodden under foot, or the stirring of a leaf in the trees, he couldn't be sure. But when he looked up around him, twirled around with his finger rigid on the trigger of the crossbow, feeling the steady weight of the spring, he noticed, off in the distance a figure.

A cloaked figure.

A chill passed through him. At first he thought it was an illusion, a trick of the light, that it was most likely a bush that had fired up his imagination. But, as he squinted harder into the gloom, he saw that it was, certainly, a cloaked figure.

A person.

A man.

And they stood there staring right at him.

Lou sniffed, glanced back over his shoulder to check out Sully's position. He wasn't anywhere in sight. And the campsite was quiet. The fire still crackled away but it was low now. And the torches would need replacing in a matter of minutes. He guessed it was close to midnight, almost time for him and Sully to raise Murch and Rut for their watch.

He caught a whiff of smoke from the fire, back at the camp, and then, somewhat out of place, the hint of cinnamon. He turned back to where the cloaked figure stood, and he felt a massive, great welt form in his throat.

Not going to be afraid now. Not this time.

He swallowed the welt in his throat back and took a step forward, listening to his trouser leg swish against the slightly damp long grass. He kept his crossbow straight before himself, pointed at the chest of the cloaked figure.

The figure reminded him of what they called the hobblesmen, the men about sixty or more that'd hobble between towns begging for money. They often wore those cloaks, usually gifted to them by some well-meaning monks—a monk's robe, that was what the cloak was.

Lou wondered if this man was confused, if he'd got himself lost out here on the plains tonight. He guessed that hobblesmen were pretty much easy game for any cursed animals that might be lurking about the plains.

Lou still kept his crossbow raised, though, he had to take care. There was no telling what or who he might run into on the plains.

A lot of the hobblesmen were drunk up to their eyelids, and some of them carried knifes, others of them—it was rumoured—were frazzled by magic.

And then he reminded himself that he was a skuller. That he had a crossbow and a sword. He could quite easily defend himself if it came down to a physical fight.

Lou was a little surprised to discover that he could speak without much effort. "You," he said. "You lost?"

The cloaked figure stood his ground, looking out from beneath that hood of the cloak, unmoved by his words.

"You hear me?" Lou said, thinking now that the man was drunk—that was most likely it.

Again, the cloaked figure remained silent.

Lou drew closer, then he glanced off to the remains of the village of Gwindermere, only then the thought occurring to him. "You . . . you weren't from here, were you?" he said. "It's terrible what's happened. Other villages too. Quagsmile, a little further back, and my village"—again that lump formed in his throat —"Endmere."

The figure made no motion or response.

Lou got closer still, so that he was only about ten or so paces away from the hobblesman. Still he couldn't see the face nestled beneath the hood of the cloak. The face was still steeped in complete shadow.

For a horrible second Lou convinced himself that the figure had no face at all. And his spine tingled. He felt his finger grow tighter on the trigger, and then he got a grip on himself. He lowered the crossbow slightly, but not all the way.

"You survived?" the figure said.

Lou was a little taken aback that the figure spoke at all. He studied the voice, a little low, a little gravelly, and there was a frailty there too. Now he was sure this was a hobblesman. He was more than likely confused about what had happened. He had probably slept in the streets of Gwindermere before venturing out onto the plains during the day.

"Yes," Lou said. "We've all survived. All of us back there at the campsite." He tilted his head back towards the others, to the fires burning themselves into cinders, then said, "You're welcome to join us, you know. I think we're heading to Ilsnare tomorrow. It seems like the whole countryside has been cursed with these fires." He dropped his voice a tone. "Some are saying that there's magic at play here."

The cloaked figure grumbled something under his breath.

"I'm sorry?" Lou said, now letting his crossbow drop in his hands, fall down to his thigh. He was probably scaring this old man stiff, what with his being dressed in skuller's uniform and pointing a weapon at him.

"You're going to Ilsnare?" the hobblesman said.

"Yes."

The cloaked figure seemed to consider this, but he made no reply.

Lou felt a slight quiver pass over his skin, his heart jiggled a little in his chest, and then he glanced back to the campsite again. His watch would be up soon, and not before time. There wasn't anything creepier than being out on the plains alone at night. Especially when you ran into hobblesmen lurking in the shadows.

"You'd better run, *skuller*."

The tone was harsh. Frosty. And it made Lou's toes curl.

Slowly Lou turned back to the cloaked figure but he was gone. "Huh?" was just about all he had time to say, as he saw a group of large beasts bounding their way through the sparse trees behind where the cloaked figure had been.

The cloaked figure had disappeared.

13

BEARS

THE SOUNDS were the first thing that registered in Lou's otherwise-numbed skull. He heard the *swish*, and the *snick* as the bears' massive claws passed through the undergrowth. They bounded toward him, about fifty or sixty paces away, but gaining every second.

Lou's grip went slick on his crossbow as he tried to pull it up, to look along the sight. And then common sense struck him, and told him one thing, and one thing plainly.

Run.

He twisted round and raced off, back towards the camp. His hearing filled with those pants, with the clobbering pounding as their paws made contact with the earth. He had had no time to count them, but he guessed there to be a whole pack of bears.

Seven? Eight? Nine? Ten? More?

Lou bounded on, screaming now at the top of his lungs, raising the camp. As he ran on, he beat his fists against the canvas of the tents, feeling the material rough against his skin. From within the tents he heard the sounds of stirring.

Across the campsite, he caught Sully's eye. He looked confused, blinking his way out of a daze, and then he looked beyond Lou, over his head, and he saw just why Lou was all riled up.

Lou watched on as Sully beat his way across the campground, already with his crossbow in hand. Sully brushed by him and let fly a few bolts into the gloom. Lou spun round, grasping his own crossbow. He chanced another glance back at the advancing pack of bears, and he saw them there, their mouths foaming, eyes bright red, like the colour a sword blade turning in a blacksmith's furnace.

Sully stood in silhouette against the frazzling-down torchlight. He worked quickly, from left to right, his elbow raised up, at right angles with his shoulder, as he fired off his bolts.

Lou saw him catch one, two. A third. Bringing them down one by one. And Lou saw the other bears note their fallen companions and fall back, hold off their brisk pace.

A wild spark of optimism flew through Lou's chest. Sully had beaten them back. He was pushing them into a retreat. However, when Sully spun round, to face up to Lou, there was no trace of a smile there, his expression was still grave, his eyes matted and yet full of action. "Raise the other skullers," he said. "Do it right now."

Lou wasted no time. He shoved his way through the survivors coming out from their tents, rubbing their eyes, mumbling questions at him. He just pushed his way through, over to the tent where Rut and Murch were sleeping.

Inside, he only found Rut, gently stirring from his blankets, like the other survivors. In the flickering torchlight that bled in from outside the tent, Lou could see the faint tear tracks lining Rut's cheeks, could hear that his sobs had shredded his voice. "What's the matter, eh?" Rut said.

"We're being overrun by bears!"

Rut squinted in the half-light, then seemed to snap out of his sleeping daze. He propped himself up, then grabbed for his trousers which lay beside him, along with his crossbow and sword.

He stumbled a couple of times as he got the right legs into the right holes of his trousers, and then, still strapping on his belt, with his crossbow dangling down off his shoulder but somehow staying put, he rushed from the tent alongside Lou.

Outside, fear was starting to take hold.

Lou cast a glance over the faces of the survivors, all of them now turned to face the bears. The survivors' mouths gaped open and some of them were crying out for help. Beyond them, Lou saw Sully still standing firm, crossbow still pointed at the bears, ready to fire off a bolt at any that chanced a step or two forward.

The bears still stood off, stalking back and forth about fifteen paces from the camp. But they no longer moved forwards.

Lou could hear their grumbling, those throaty roars knocking about the backs of their mouths. Everything sat on a hair trigger, ready to fly apart at any second. Lou also saw the bear corpses, four of them now, it seemed that Sully had taken out another bear while he'd been off fetching Rut.

The bears started to move for the flanks, to spread out. Right away Lou could see just what they were planning.

They were trying to surround the camp.

With only a glance at Rut, they scattered in separate directions, the two of them heading right through the camp, and out to the perimeter, so that they'd see off any charge.

Lou felt his heart rapping against his ribcage, and in his hysteria he thought about Syre. He hadn't seen her, back at the camp. And now her face flashed up in his mind, made him want to scramble desperately back to check on her. But, in his rational mind, he knew that he needed to stand his ground, else the bears would find a way in.

And the bears would get them all.

And so he held up his crossbow to his eye, and peered along it.

Two bears broke off from the main group, and pawed their way towards him.

Lou glanced away from his crossbow for a second, to look over to Sully. But he was occupied with his own affairs.

Three of the bears were now roaring at him, taking turns to stand on their hind legs, those bright red eyes of theirs flashing with rage.

Rut, on the other side of the camp, had his own two bears to deal with.

Lou turned back to his bears, peered along the crossbow sight, and feeling his whole body tremble, let fly.

The bolt skittered through the air with a *whistle* following the displaced air. He watched it, gawping, as it flew into the earth at one of the bear's hind paws. Both bears stared down at the bolt lodged in the earth, then looked back to Lou. They broke into a run, headed straight for him.

Lou felt his crossbow slip from his hands, heard the meshing of the mechanism, and the clacking of the bolts as it hit the earth. Without thinking, all his attention being filled by those twin pairs of fire-bright eyes, he reached for the hilt of his sword and drew it out.

The sword felt almost impossibly heavy, lunky, held down by his side. That stench of metal filled his nostrils, and seemed to hollow out his mouth. And those bears pounding ever closer to him made his heart jig twice as fast. Their pants filled his ears, and yet he told himself that this was his time. That he was going to save everyone.

One of the bears leaped at him.

He clasped the sword in his fist, and then swung it through the air, eyes closed. At the same time, the motion sent him to his knees, and he felt the slightly damp earth through the fabric of his trousers.

He only knew he'd made contact when he heard the whimper. So much like a dog's whimper. Like a street dog that's been kicked by the butcher for trying to trot off with a bunch of sausages.

And when he looked back he saw the bear lying behind him, in a great fury lump of blood-smeared fur.

Motionless.

Lou squeezed hold of the sword again then eyed the next bear, holding back now, having stopped in its tracks after it'd seen Lou had downed its companion. He waited for him, feeling the full force of his breathing, his chest rising against the underside of his tunic. The sweat smeared in his hair.

The bear rushed him.

Lou side-stepped, a move he'd tried several times as a kid, when he'd snuck into bull fields, got the bull all riled up, then taken turns with his friends to avoid it. This time, though, it was different.

Instead of rolling off to one side, to safety, he stood his ground and thrust his sword down, *hard*, into the bear's back. He watched the blade sink into the hard flesh and then stick there. He felt the hilt slip from between his fingers, and the bear stumble to one side, taking his sword with it.

Lou stood there, unarmed now. He eyed his crossbow. It was about a dozen steps to his right, just where he'd dropped it. He turned his attention back to the bear.

It jerked its head back, as if trying to dislodge the sword from its hide with its mouth. Its eyes glowed like a pair of red-hot coals Then, with an enormous effort, it rose onto its hind legs and swiped at the sword with its claws.

But it failed to make contact.

It let loose a huge roar, which sent a tingling sensation dancing through all Lou's muscles, and turned his gut to jelly water.

The bear rose to its hind legs again and made another swipe for the hilt of the sword.

Again it missed.

And this time, it toppled over onto its side and rested there, its whole form rapidly rising and falling with its dying breaths.

Lou stood staring at what he'd done for several seconds. Only when he heard the shout, someone shouting out his name, did he think to look away.

Across the camp, he saw that both Sully and Rut were facing down six bears. Sully kept them back with his crossbow, rapidly firing off bolts into their joints, apparently targeting the undersides of their chins, their necks, while Rut ran in with his sword and thrust it about, looking to do all the damage he could.

Lou raced over to the bear he'd killed, his head humming, and his fear long-forgotten, then he stooped over and tore his sword out of its carcass. As he ran on he thought about how those bears he'd downed were like a distant memory now that he had to face up to these six.

The survivors were long from being saved.

He stood alongside Sully and held his sword down at his side. He looked for some way in for himself, a way that he might get involved in the fight. He watched those gleaming eyes, those mouths yawning open, trying to get a bite of Rut, but too slow for Sully's crossbow bolts.

Right as a bear attempted to take a chunk out of Rut's thigh, Lou watched as Sully sent a bolt skidding through the air and into that bear's brain. It toppled over onto its side and lay there dead.

Sully slipped Lou a sidelong glance then said, through gritted teeth, in a gruff voice, "Go on, then, whatcha waitin' for?"

Lou rushed forwards, holding his sword out before him, just like he saw Rut do, then he flung himself into the bear standing on the periphery, and buried the blade in the bear's neck.

A spurt of warm blood cascaded through the air and splattered against Lou's cheek. He reached to wipe it away with his free hand as, with the other, he slipped the blade back out.

He turned back to look at Rut, and saw him facing up to two bears.

Together with Rut, they drove the bears back. The bears rose onto their hind legs and swiped at them with their shredding claws, but they caught only air.

And metal.

Soon enough, he and Rut had downed them.

Looking around, Lou saw that it was all over.

That they'd won.

There were no more bears to come.

He felt the blood buzz through his veins, and that sick, metallic taste in his mouth. He could smell that musky scent of the bears, and that sharp, toxic stench that he knew could only be associated with black magic. The curses loosening themselves from the bears in death.

He listened to his breaths echo about his chest, as they stoppered slightly at the back of his throat. He slowed his breathing, told himself to relax, that they'd won the battle.

He looked over Sully and Rut.

They were all equally as exhausted. The two of them still clutching their weapons, their crossbows and their swords. He looked beyond them, back to the campsite.

Among those grim faces, spread with shock, he saw his sis, Syre, standing among them.

She was wrapped in her blanket, had it draped round her shoulders. Her lips were slightly parted and he saw that she still clutched that book to her chest. He shifted away from Sully and Rut, sheathed his sword then headed towards her.

He reached out and touched her shoulder, tried to get her to turn to look at him, maybe even to say something. But she just kept up that stare, into the middle-distance. "Sy?" he said, his voice sounding thick and rich now, full of confidence because of his kills.

She just stared on.

He looked to the book she held in her hands, and reached for her fingers. He managed to unclasp them, one by one, from the cover. He saw that she'd been holding it so tight over the course of the last day or so that the cover was now indented with her fingertips, those dents forever burrowed into the soft leather.

He held the book out before him, glanced over the title: *A Practical Understanding of Dark Magic*.

A tingle ran through him. He felt his hands shake just a little. Never would he have imagined them having something like this in the house. He glanced back to Syre, still transfixed by something in the distance, above the slaughtered cursed bears. "Was this ma's book?" he said.

She kept on staring away from him.

"Where'd you get this?"

It was no use. She just wouldn't look away from that spot in mid-air. And then, gently and with infinite care, she reached out to him, brushed her hand against the book.

He knew that she wanted it back. That it really didn't matter at all what it contained. She just wanted it for comfort. And so he let it go.

She took it back from him, crushed it back to her chest.

He felt a little emptied, like his adrenalin following his kills was beginning to ebb out of his system. And his body was starting to chill.

Rut called to him.

Lou turned his head to look, and saw that he was calling him on, that Sully had already stalked ahead into the gloom. He guessed that their work wasn't quite done yet, that they'd want to do a proper check of the periphery before giving up their stand against the cursed bears. And so, with a heavy heart, he squeezed hold of Syre's shoulder, her still staring off into the trees, over the bear carcasses, and he went after the other skullers.

Lou hustled to keep up with them. He felt the cool night air flushing the sweat from his pores, carrying it away on the breeze. He could smell the earth now, and taste its cleansing effect as he put distance between himself and the downed bears. In the near distance he heard that all too familiar grumbling.

And, instinctively, he knew it was another bear.

14

A FALLEN SOLDIER

LOU FELT his heart bounce in his chest, his hands go clammy once more. He unsheathed his sword, the steady weight of it already feeling more intimate, more familiar, to his touch. He had killed two bears on his own. Another six with Rut and Sully. He had shed his fear, that uncontrollable trembling which seemed to lock up his muscles and make him clumsy.

Now he was ready to be a warrior.

And he would never more be afraid.

He breathed in that musky scent, carrying on the breeze, tasted that sour tang at the back of his tongue, and he kept his eyes sharp, his attention fixed on Sully and Rut as they ploughed forwards in the direction of the growling.

They passed through a few trees, and then they saw the bear's flanks, the bear half-hidden behind a mud bank. That was when Lou realised he could hear another sound too. Not just the growling of the bear, the ripping of flesh in its jaws, but he could also here the near-muted moans of a man.

As he stepped forward, carefully picking his way along the foliage-strewn forest floor, keeping up with Sully and Rut as they went on their way just as carefully, he gripped his sword tight and prepared to bring it down on their enemy.

Soon the bear came into view before them. He was focussed down on what he was eating, the person he had pressed up against the side of the muddy bank.

Lou didn't wait for either Rut or Sully, he simply rushed forward and, with a flick of the blade that was already becoming increasingly familiar to him, he thrust the blade down into the back of the bear, listening to the *snick* and *crunch* as he plunged it through the bear's hide.

This time he was quick and he retrieved the blade swiftly, brought it back, ready for the bear to spin round and go at him with its jaws.

But this time there'd be no resistance.

The bear let out an elongated, rumbling moan then rolled over on its side. As it lay there, downed, it twitched several times over, and Lou saw the blood pulsing out from the wound he'd inflicted. Saw the bear breathing its last, the curse leaving its bloodstream.

Next his attention moved to the man they'd saved—the man Lou had feared it would be.

Lying there, on his back, his stomach ripped open, the rags of his tunic soaked with black blood, was Murch.

Lou felt his heart lodge in his throat and, almost subconsciously, he returned his sword to its sheath, then stepped forward to see to his dying boss.

It was Sully who broke them out of their daze, their staring down at their boss, Murch, lying there, bleeding out his guts. He ordered Rut and Lou to go off and fetch fresh water. Lou jumped to his orders, as did Rut. It seemed that, with all the drama they'd had that night, they were quickly approaching the limits for their trauma.

They needed someone to order them about, to tell them just what they had to do.

Lou got to thinking that soon he might need someone to remind him to breathe.

Lou and Rut found a fresh-water stream, a burbling creek, just a few paces away. They both filled up their canisters with the water, then returned to where Sully stood with Murch. Even without needing to draw close, not even needing to look Sully in the face, let alone look down, Lou knew what had happened. That Murch was dead. It was the smell, that faintly musky, bloody, earthy stench.

He was learning to know it well.

The three skullers stood over their downed boss for several minutes, Lou fancied all of them staring at his parted lips, at his lolled open eyes. That scar occupying most of his face. Lou thought about how he'd grown up with the man keeping him safe all his life, and thought about how little he'd really known about him, and then he thought about how Murch had taken him in, made him one of his own, when he'd been truly desperate.

Sully spoke in his low drawl, eyes still firmly fixed to Murch's corpse. "We'd be better off burying him somewhere close by, keeping this secret from the rest. It'll only make everyone panic."

Slowly he turned his head to look at Rut and Lou. "Better to keep it between us, yeah?"

Lou turned this over in his mind. He thought about all that Murch had done, how, if this had somehow been a just world, then Murch truly would've been celebrated, that they would've all come together to celebrate just all he'd done to keep them safe.

But the way it was, he knew that the world just wasn't just.

Hadn't he, just like the rest of his fellow villagers, ignored most of the efforts of the skullers, at best slipped them glances in the early mornings or late evenings, at most a subtle, glum-faced nod.

They were an accepted necessity.

A sign of the cursed times they were living through.

But that shouldn't have meant dying in obscurity.

Skullers were on the light side of the world. Protectors. Comfort-givers. And, Lou considered, that he was truly proud that he himself was one.

. . . Or that one day he might be accepted as one.

They did just what Sully suggested. The three of them digging out a shallow grave with nothing but the blades of their swords and a few rocks. It took them till the morning light licked the horizon, but they got it done. The grave was a shallow one, no more than coming up to the height of Lou's knees.

But it would have to do in times like these.

They marked it with three large stones, arranged in a triangle, according to the customs of the region.

Lou promised to himself, staring down at that stirred-up earth, that one day he would return, come back here and give Murch a proper burial. He was determined that he would be remembered in the way he, and his work, deserved.

The procession back to the campsite was a sombre one. None of them said anything about what they'd just had to do. And as they returned, Lou saw the survivors still all standing about in the early morning light, obviously waiting for them to return. They were waiting for their protectors, as they well might.

Lou looked for Syre, automatically, but he couldn't see her anywhere. He guessed she'd returned back to her own tent, with that book of hers.

The one which'd been called: *A Practical Understanding of Dark Magic.*

Just thinking about it sent a chill up his spine.

15

ON CAPITAL ROAD

THEY BROKE CAMP soon after daybreak. Lou felt his heart sink down to his gut as they headed up the hill, back to the main road. He felt his muscles twitching with his sleepless night, and his mouth still tasted of the blood of those cursed bears. He tried to wash it all away with several mouthfuls of water, but to no avail. Even the fresh morning air didn't offer much in the way of rejuvenation. He listened to the trudge of the boots of their group of survivors, to the rustle of their clothing as they all made their way along.

He stayed at the side of the horse carrying Syre, leading it by the reins. He clasped those leather straps tight in his hand, telling himself that no matter what happened there was no chance that he would let go.

About as much chance of him letting go as of her letting go of that book she clutched to her chest.

Sully led the front of the group, and Lou could see him at the front, leading their snaking procession. Rut brought up the rear. Looking back, Lou noticed that Rut kept glancing back over his shoulder, as if there might be some cursed bear about to sneak up on them—as if the cursed animals might've changed their mind about coming out in the daytime.

Still, Lou had to admit to himself that he did feel a little on edge about it, even if he did tell himself that he'd exorcised the fear about the whole thing.

Now he knew he could kill.

And under duress.

They made Capital Road soon enough, just after midday. Lou felt the sturdy bricks beneath his feet, and he thought about how this road had all been possible thanks to the corn they'd picked out in the fields, all those yields they'd brought in, it was all wrapped up in this fine work. And, in a way, they were walking across all those yields from down all those years.

For the first time, Lou really saw the results, first hand, of that 'good, honest work' all the working hands chatted about.

Sully drove them on at a brisk pace, for obvious reasons wanting to get them to the outskirts before the sun came down, to where the city barricades began. Once they got inside the barricades, Lou was sure that they'd be safe.

From what he'd pieced together from what he'd heard off other working hands, the guards that held the barricades controlled the entry and exit, flushed out the cursed animals using a series of complicated gating systems.

In fact, despite everything else that had happened to them, Lou couldn't help being a little excited about going to Ilsnare.

It only served to make him sombre, to make him want to curl

up into a ball and weep, to think that this opportunity had cost him his ma and pa.

But he couldn't indulge his emotions any longer.

Now he was a skuller.

While they'd been on the trail, Sully had pretty much had them stopping every couple of hours or so, so that they could all get in some rest, take on some water, away from the relentless slog onwards.

But, as the sun dipped on the horizon, there was no sign of Sully so much as breaking his pace. Then again, as Lou looked around, he saw that most of their group looked apprehensive, their faces sketched with worry lines, lips pressed together tightly, and Lou knew that they had to make the barricades before sundown just to put everyone's mind at rest.

As Lou trudged onwards, leading the reins of Syre's horse, something in the distance caught his eye. It was a sparkle, what could only be the reflection of the harsh sunlight. And in that second he knew that he was seeing a glass spire. The first hint of The Crystal City.

His heart jigged up to his throat, and before he got a hold on his excitement, he called out and pointed, and soon enough the whole group of their survivors were staring in that direction.

For the first time since they'd escaped the rubble of Endmere, the survivors broke out into something approaching excited conversation.

Looking round, Lou saw people with a fresh colour to their faces, their cheeks plumper, their eyes rounder. And he knew that he too was showing off those signs. He was just as excited as they were.

Their pace seemed to increase to double-time, with them all

winding their way along Capital Road. Soon enough, the barricades came into sight, a great big, black wall before them, at least the height of ten or fifteen men. And those glass spires shone beyond them, sparkling in the light of the setting sun, until they were totally consumed by the looming walls of the barricade before them.

The walls were pit-black.

Once, a long time ago now, Lou remembered when a pair of hobblesmen had come to Endmere. They weren't like the normal sort, which was to say half-barmy, no these ones were artisans, and they talked about where they'd come from—somewhere off in the Sable Mountains, from a mining village near there known as Dweldwock.

Painters, both of them.

They'd travelled from village to village selling their paintings during the summers, and in the winters they'd go back off home and get back to their painting.

It had been one of those rare nights—those nights that Lou could count on one hand—where he'd found himself swindled by a fellow working hand, most likely Eirk or Poels, into coming down to *The Mocker's Pit*, 'just for a half pint.' And of course, he'd been hoodwinked into several more.

Lou could still taste the vomit at the back of his throat, still feel the sting of it, and still remember the stench of his guts in his nose from all the puking he'd done that night.

But those two men, they'd shown off their paintings, all of them done in charcoal. Different shades of it. Some almost grey, some jet-black. And he remembered the very deepest of the blacks that they'd reserved for the mine pits themselves. And when, in a somewhat drunken stupor, Lou had asked just what they called that shade, they'd told him, their voices a touch awed, that it was known as 'pit-black.'

And that was just the colour of the walls of the barricades before them.

In fact, Lou wondered whether they'd got the rocks for the walls out of the Sable Mountains themselves. Perhaps those hobblesmen had helped dig them out themselves.

As they drew closer, Lou watched the winding Capital Road approaching the large, equally pit-black gates. These gates glistened slightly in the setting sun. As they headed onwards, they entered the shadow of the gates, and Lou couldn't help but stare upwards in awe, at them towering above.

As he walked on, still in awe of the gates, taking in the pit-black colour, thinking of those hobblesmen that'd visited Endmere years before, his mind flashed back to the night before.

His memories were already a little sluggish, delirious from lack of sleep, but he did remember one thing.

The hobblesman who'd stood out there, who'd . . . *warned* them about the impending bears. Had that been what he'd done, though? Had he really raised the warning?

Or had he just told him that they were coming?

Lou thought on the matter harder, those pit-black barricades drawing closer and closer, almost seeming to consume them as they got nearer. The effect was almost hypnotising. He felt his mind zoning out, and the sleepiness leaving his mind frayed and torn.

The hobblesman had just stood there, wearing the hood, and then he'd disappeared.

If the hobblesman hadn't warned Lou then he supposed he would've seen the bears in any case. And that made him wonder if the hobblesman had had something to do with the animals coming.

Perhaps he'd summoned them in some way.

Even Lou, as a green, *rookie* skuller, knew that attacks from cursed bears were exceptionally uncommon. So why had they come last night, that particular night? Had they sensed easy prey? That was possible, of course. And, as he reached the end of his wonderings, as their group reached a halt at the gates, with Sully still at the head of the group, Lou knew that he was much better off leaving this to ask Sully later on, raising the matter with him.

Sully would know.

Sully was now, to all intents and purposes, the head skuller among them.

Lou watched on as the great, grand doors rolled back from their position. He could hear the grinding of the mechanism, someway back, coming from deep within the barricades, and then, just like that, they swarmed their way in through the gates.

Lou just stared all about him as he passed through those enormous gates. He swivelled to look above him, to the ramparts of the barricades, and he saw the guards staring down at them.

Each guard held a bow, an arrow already notched in. Lou took in their uniforms, a kind of wispy grey colour, now that he thought of it, the colour of The Crystal City itself, or at least what he'd glimpsed of it from along Capital Road.

Never before had he seen such fine uniforms, and, at the same time, he noted the stern expressions of the half dozen guards manning the ramparts, peering down on them, not looking likely to let go of their bows and arrows any time soon.

Once they'd all got inside the barricades, Lou noticed that they'd only passed into an area just inside the walls. Before them stood another pair of much smaller doors. And they were firmly sealed.

As Lou turned back, he caught the motion of the main doors, the ones they'd just passed through, sliding shut behind them. When he heard that steady *thunk* he knew they were safe from the plains, from the cursed animals that would soon rampage about the countryside.

He glanced about him, taking it in. He supposed that this was a kind of screening area.

Below his feet was the brick of Capital Road. He looked to Sully for some sort of a cue about what was going to happen next. Sully met Lou's eye briefly, then turned his attention to the smaller doors before them. But that wasn't where the voice came from. The voice came from back up on the ramparts, from one of the guards.

"Maun Fleeter, Royal Guards! Identify yourselves!"

Lou peered up at the guard who'd spoken. He saw him peering down at them, like all the others, with his bow clasped in his hands, and an arrow notched into it. That made Lou uneasy. And it dawned on him that this area, whatever it was, would make them sitting ducks for those arrows.

He guessed that was just what these guards had in mind.

Sully glanced over the group, perhaps wondering if Lou or Rut was going to respond to the guard. But Lou glanced back at him with assurance in his gaze, that now Sully was well and truly the leader of their group. Besides, if Lou had said something back to the guard, he might've got them into deep trouble.

Sully swallowed hard, even from several paces away Lou could see that. From what Lou had seen of Sully so far, he knew that he wasn't all that fond of speaking. But now he would have to shout. "We've come from Endmere!" Sully said, clasping his hands around his mouth to project his voice. "The villages, out there, on the plains! Several have caught fire and burned to the ground!"

The guard tilted his head and cast another glare over their group, then he looked back to Sully. "What caused the fire?" the guard bellowed back.

Again, Sully looked in Lou's direction, as if he wanted some sort of reinforcement, but he did just fine on his own, or so Lou thought, as he spoke back. "We don't know!"

The guard looked off to one of his colleagues and they consulted about something in voices that were muffled up there on the ramparts.

Lou guessed that this was a good arrangement for them. Most likely they could hear every word uttered down in this screening area, while those down in the screening area, like Lou and the survivors now were, wouldn't hear anything they'd say.

Before Lou could think things through any more, he heard the creak of the two smaller doors yawning open. And the group as a whole shuffled towards the opening.

16

INSIDE THE CRYSTAL CITY

THE SETTING SUN caught all the buildings before them in a great, bright orange luminescence. The brightness of it all made Lou's eyes sting, and he had to shield his eyes from the glare coming off the glass. Slowly, his eyes grew accustomed and he could make out the forms of the buildings before him.

It was just like all his dreams. The buildings grew up out of the cobbled streets in elegant, arced constructions. He followed their curved lines as they towered up above him, into the darkening blue sky above. He breathed in the smells, no stench of sewage like there had always been upon entering Endmere, everything about the place was fresh, like it had been greased up with lemons and limes.

In the near distance he could hear the light thrumming of a guitar, or some other instrument he couldn't identify. Back in Endmere they only had few musicians in the village, some who could play flutes or a drum. Only when hobblesmen passed through Endmere did they ever get anyone with real musical talent.

But now, standing here in Ilsnare, he knew that The Crystal City had all the culture in the world.

Up ahead, though, he saw the fence, keeping them back for the time being. And then, at the gate to the fence, a pair of guards. They wore the same uniforms as the ones up on the ramparts, back at the barricade, and Lou wondered if they were the same guards.

His question was answered almost right away when he recognised the voice of one of them, speaking to Sully at the front of the group. Seeing that he was wearing the uniform of a skuller—that he *was* a skuller—he decided he'd better stand alongside him. So he shuffled his way along the group and stood beside Sully, waiting there patiently.

Maun, a member of the Royal Guard, as he'd introduced himself back at the barricade, stood stern-faced with his bow slung over his shoulder. He was much shorter than he'd seemed up on the ramparts. Perhaps about a head smaller than Sully, and a head and shoulders shorter than Lou.

From looking at him, how Maun's eyes darted between the two of them, Lou knew that he didn't trust either of them, that they'd have to work for his trust. "You'll have to change before we let you enter the city," Maun said. "Can't have you going about here in *those* uniforms. Only the Royal Guards can wear uniform in the city. King's orders."

Sully grunted.

Maun glanced to Lou, then to Rut who'd just shown up at his shoulder. Then he looked back to Sully. "What did you say about the villages? That they're burned down?"

Lou saw this as his opportunity to get more involved, and so he decided to speak up. "Three villages," he said. "Endmere, Quagsmile and Gwindermere. All of them gone."

Maun pouted. "Sounds a little odd, don't you think?"

Again, neither Rut or Sully seemed to want to speak up, so Lou took it upon himself. "People talked about magic. Said that magic might've been at play."

Even as he said it, Lou could feel both Rut and Sully turning in on him, glowering at him. And he knew that he'd said just the wrong thing.

Maun, too, grew uneasy. He took a step back, slipped the other Royal Guard standing at his shoulder a sidelong glance, before looking back over them. "Like I said. Gotta take those uniforms off before you enter the city." He stepped away from them. "This zone's known as Taldry, and we'll get you all sorted out with temporary residencies as soon as possible. Where you can get those uniforms off." He nodded to the horses too. "I'll have my men take those off to the stables, get them taken care of." Then he cast a look up at the sky, the light fading away now. "Better not to be out in the streets at this time. When the mist descends."

Lou felt a twinge at the base of his spine. Everything about this place, with the buildings, and the smells, and the music in the air, just seemed almost impossible to believe. And yet he picked up on the sinister undercurrent present here too, and he'd almost forgotten about the mist that descended on the place at dusk and dawn. It had almost slipped his mind completely.

But now his mind was very much back there, and he wanted to get out of the mist's way as soon as possible.

～

They followed Maun down a series of crooked streets. Lou took in the storefronts, all shutting up at speed. He watched an elderly woman, with her silver-grey hair coiled right down to the pit of her stomach. She was carefully but swiftly plucking the apples off her stall and placing them in a wooden crate. She cast them a glance as they passed by. And Lou caught a whiff of that rotten, apple mulch smell.

That reminded him of being back on Old Man Junth's farm, when one day they'd gone to work in the orchard, and at lunch they'd all eaten apples off the trees. That seemed a long time ago now. A happier time. Before his whole world had been turned upside down.

After they'd carried on around several corners, trudged their way up countless cobbled streets, Lou felt the soles of his feet aching. He wanted a bucket of warm water and maybe half an hour just to get some rest, then he could start again.

Already he was looking forward to a long night of fulfilling sleep. And yet, at the same time, he felt so much activity buzzing through him, all the new experience of this city—The Crystal City —just begging to be explored. But, as he well knew, his primary duty was to protect Syre. To keep her close. And there was no way he could do that effectively if he was staggering about like a man half-dead from lack of sleep.

They reached a large, iron-cast door, and Maun leaned over and tapped it twice with his knuckles. Then he glanced back over them, nodded, and watched them file past him and into the place. Lou looked over his shoulder and saw Maun counting them into the building, before shutting the door behind him.

Inside, there were some torches hanging off the walls, their flames bouncing an orange glow about the place. The room was a square shape, and the windows were set high up above them, at least, Lou thought, the height of five or six men above.

Suddenly, from all around, Lou sensed motion. And, before he had a chance to react, he felt someone seize hold of his sword, and then his crossbow. Before he knew it, he was completely disarmed. He pivoted around to see that the same had happened to Sully and Rut.

Maun stood at the door, his arms folded across his chest, his same grave expression. "Like I said, no uniforms allowed in the city. No weapons either."

Lou watched on as the guard who had taken his sword and crossbow, laid them out on the floor at the opposite wall. The guards then stood to attention, six of them, their backs straight and their chins tilted at such an angle that they wouldn't have to look anyone in the eye.

Lou glanced to Sully and Rut, trying to ascertain just what they were going to do next. It seemed, to Lou, that they simply had no choice other than to do whatever it was that the Royal Guards said they had to do.

Maun pursed his lips as if considering how he would phrase what he had to say next, then he said it. "I'm afraid this is standard procedure for new arrivals to Ilsnare. It's part of our duty to ensure that the city remains disease-free, and that every new entrant is duly registered."

This time Sully did speak up, spinning round, his eyes ablaze as he looked over Maun. "It wasn't like this last time I was here. We could come and go as we pleased."

Maun smiled a little grimly. "Things have changed. Times have changed. Now we're more cautious. We have to take more care." Then he increased the volume of his voice as he addressed everyone. "Each of you shall be inspected over the course of the next twenty-four hours before you are let loose in Ilsnare. As long as you cooperate it should be a painless process."

And with that, Maun waved to the guards once more. They strode forward in those grey uniforms of theirs, and Lou only realised at the last moment that two of them were coming for him. Before he had the chance to react, they seized him beneath his armpits, and dragged him off in the direction of another room.

As Lou approached the door, he managed a glance back over his shoulder, to see Sully and Rut being treated the same way, each of them also with a pair of guards. And then he looked to Syre, that book, *A Practical Understanding of Dark Magic*, still clutched to her chest.

If he thought crying out would've done any good then he would've done it. But he had the sense to hold his consul. And with that, the two guards whisked him from the room and away from her.

Perhaps forever.

17

GAOLED IN THE CRYSTAL CITY

THE GAOL CELL was ripe with stale air. There were no windows Lou could see. He sat slumped on the floor with his back pressed up against the brick wall and listened to the gentle breathing of his cellmates, of Rut and Sully. His mouth felt all dry too, and he thought about how he hadn't had a drink of water in several hours now. He'd thought that once they'd got into Ilsnare they'd be able to drink all they wanted. But no.

As Lou sat there, his head still spinning from the rough treatment they'd got off the guards, he tried to piece things back together again in his mind. They hadn't taken their uniforms off them. Yet. He wondered if they might be coming back soon to do that, to issue them with whatever clothes they were supposed to wear in Ilsnare.

Lou glanced about the cell again, his eyes coming to rest on Sully, he remembered just what he was supposed to tell him. Despite his aching body, his bones seeming to complain that he was sitting up rather than lying down, he shucked the weariness from his voice and faced up to him. "Sully?" Lou said.

Sully glanced over to him, those black eyes of his, and that hair slicked right down the back of his neck, glistening just a little in the weak torchlight in their cell.

Lou continued. "There's something I've got to tell you."

As Lou met Sully's eye, he noticed Rut stirring too, coming out of his own daze. He guessed that was for the best with what he had to say. One of them would be able to put him right, one of them would be able to tell him whether or not he had gone totally mad. "Back there, back at Gwindermere, when we set up camp, before the bears came, I had a run-in with a hobblesman."

"A hobblesman?" Rut said, raising his eyebrows.

Lou nodded and stared down at his tunic, still drench with sweat, in thought. "Yeah, in a cloak and everything." He strained his mind, trying to work out just what they'd said to one another —what the hobblesman had said to him.

Lou looked back over to Rut and Sully. "I asked him if he was okay, he seemed pretty stunned, didn't really seem to know just what was going on. Didn't reply to me. I told him we were going to Ilsnare, asked him if he wanted to come with us, where he'd be safe. And then, . . . and then . . ." Again, Lou found himself adrift in thought, trying to get the wording just right. "He said, 'You'd better run, skuller.'" He stared long and hard at Rut and Sully. "And then he just disappeared, faded into the air. And the bears stomped out from behind him, from out in the woods."

The cell descended into silence for a while.

Somewhere close by, Lou could hear the *drip-drip* of a pipe leaking, and the air in the place seemed to get thicker, moister, with each one of their exhales. He tasted their mixed odours getting up his nose, sticking at the back of his mouth. A shudder passed over his skin.

On instinct, he clasped his arms across his chest to ward off . . . well, it wasn't a chill, more of a . . . a sense of apprehension. They still had no idea what was going to happen to them and talking about magic wasn't doing much to help.

It was Rut that spoke first, his blond hair and blue eyes looking the most out of place here amongst all of them. His jolly, rounded figure, too, seemed to grate with the irrepressibly dank and grey cell. And there was no brightness in his voice, none of that jubilance which Lou had noted when they'd first met. "You think it was a mage?"

Lou thought that over for a moment or two. Of course, all throughout the Kingdom of Shellacnass, people talked about mages, and wise women, all of that. But no one had ever actually seen one, or that was what it seemed to Lou.

And, looking from the quiet contemplation of Sully, as he sat slumped there staring between his knees, to the slight look of confusion on Rut's face as he stared back, Lou knew that he'd made himself out to be some sort of crazy person. That his childish sighting would forever mark both Rut and Sully's judgement of him. Even after what he'd shown in the battle back at Gwindermere, with the cursed bears.

Lou met those blazing blue eyes of Rut's again, then nodded in reply.

Rut broke off eye contact and his eyeballs swivelled in their sockets to take in the roof above their heads.

The manky mould that grew up there looked like fur to Lou. And he could almost feel the texture of it on his tongue, almost breath in its earthiness.

When Rut spoke again, he kept on staring up at the roof. "You know, when I was young I remember coming across something quite similar." He poked his tongue out of the corner of his mouth. "Was on the way home after being out in the fields, one day in early summer, or something like it, and as I dropped off the cart, I remember seeing a cloaked figure, right outside the stone wall of . . . of"—he took a quick gulp, swallowing back the tears that Lou knew were lingering there—"Quagsmile."

Rut looked back over at Lou, while Sully kept up his steady contemplation of the ground between his knees. "Anyway, I did just like you, I asked him if he was all right. Remember that he was swaying about quite a bit, and I got the feeling that he'd been in some public house, some tavern, somewhere along the road."

Rut's lips straightened up into a frown. "And I remember really clear, like, reaching out for him, laying my hand on his shoulder even, and then, just as my fingertips came into contact with his cloak he . . . he just disappeared."

Rut flashed his eyes and then, suddenly and violently, unclasped his fist. "Just like that, right into thin air, if you can imagine it."

Lou felt his shoulders lighten just a little. He was glad that Rut had confided in him. At least there would be two of them in this cell that were crazy now, that Lou wouldn't feel so alone.

The two of them turned to look at Sully, still staring down at the ground, as if half-expecting him to have a story of his own about a mysterious cloaked figure—a hobblesman that had simply slipped away into thin air. But Sully remained perfectly still, offering nothing. And Lou knew that he had nothing to tell them. He could only speculate as to what he thought of them now.

What kinds of fools he'd painted them to be.

Lou guessed that he must've succumbed to sleep at some point in the course of the night. When he woke up, he saw that the torch had gone out, but he knew it was day by the light which trickled in from beneath the iron gaol door. He examined the light's tangerine glow, was transfixed by it for the longest time, before he noticed that Sully too was awake, and that he was staring right at him, those twin black eyes of his scoping him out the whole time.

Lou felt a shudder pass up his spine. But he shucked off the feeling just as quickly, pinning on a smile. They could just about make each other out in the gloom of the cell. "Sleep well?" Lou said, trying to lighten the mood.

Lou saw that, beside Sully, sprawled out on his back with his mouth wide open, that Rut was snoring.

Sully pursed his lips, then looked to the door. He nodded to it. "I've been listening to things out there. Heard a lot of boots passing by, crunching up and down."

"What do you think they're gonna do with us?"

Sully remained perfectly still, still staring at the door as if it might be about to give him the answer to eternal life. "Dunno."

Lou wanted to know more, of course he did, but, at the same time, he knew that now was the time for him to sit back and wait. Sully was a thinker. He never acted rashly. Lou had learned that in just the few days they'd spent together—these few days which felt like years.

Rut snivelled, and a bubble of snot formed out of his left nostril and then burst. He made a strange jabbering noise with his lips, and then, one lid at a time, he opened his eyes and slowly took stock of Lou and Sully, both of them staring at him.

Lou couldn't help giving a slight chuckle. Looking at Rut's dazed state, seeing him waking up like that in such an abrupt way, and with a bursting bubble of snot, it was too much for him.

When he cast a glance over at Sully, he was that he too was smiling—if only very faintly. But considering that it was Sully, it might as well have been a cheek-splitting grin.

"Where'a'wha?" Rut said, prising himself off the floor on his elbow.

But that was all the time he had to recover, because Lou heard those crunching boots carrying their way down the corridor outside the cell and, seconds later, the iron door burst open, first creaking on its hinges and then rebounding off the wall with a resounding *clang*.

Maun Fleeter, of the Royal Guards, stood there darkening the doorway.

He wore his crisp, ethereal-grey uniform. Today he wore no weapons, although Lou was sure that there would be a guard out there in the corridor, hidden away, ready to bring a scimitar down on anyone who dared stir up trouble.

Lou had no intention of stirring up trouble.

"Moving you," Maun said, without bothering with a greeting.

They were, after all, Lou supposed, technically prisoners at this moment in time.

Maun snapped his fingers and three guards, previously hidden behind him, out in the corridor, appeared before them. The guards moved efficiently and cleanly, this time taking the trouble to cuff each of their prisoners.

Lou stared as one of the guards approached him and pressed those iron bracelets to his wrists, the freezing-cold metal sending tremors through his bones, and then he watched as that same guard put another pair of cuffs around his ankles, before attaching it to a chain which he himself took. "Where're the others?" Lou said to Maun.

"Somewhere else."

"My sis," Lou said, feeling those words dry up in his mouth. "Is she okay?"

"I don't know which one is, uh, your '*sis*.'"

Lou glanced about swiftly, and then settled back on Maun. "Where're you taking us?"

Maun smiled weakly. "You'll see."

'You'll see,' turned out to be a trip in a cart through the immaculate streets of Ilsnare. Even though he was bound and all the people out on the streets stared at them all there in the gaoler's cart, Lou couldn't help but savour that *clickety-clack* of the cart-wheels as they passed over the cobblestones, and the stormy exhales of the horses. He caught a whiff of the air scented with all sorts of smells—herbs that he had never smelled before, let alone would have been able to name.

It was all so . . . exotic, and new, to him.

Lou looked to Rut who sat bound before him, the soles of their boots touching as they both sat in the base of the cart. He saw that Rut was just as enraptured with Ilsnare as he was, just as keen to drink it all in.

Sully, though, typically, was unmoved.

Sully sat slouched beside Lou, and not for one second did he tear his gaze away from the shoulder of the driver of the cart, of the road ahead, the cobblestones stretching out before them.

Lou wondered what he might be thinking, and was on the point of asking, when before them, an elderly lady, about seventy or so, rushed out into the middle of the road.

Her hair was on fire.

She let loose a blood-curdling scream.

The horses reared up, but the driver soon got them back under control.

Lou glanced about the cart to see that their escort, the three guards that had accompanied them from the gaol, held their scimitars across their chests, and that they were approaching the elderly woman.

Looking around, he noted that they were alone. That they were unguarded. He slipped Sully a sidelong glanced, trying to work out whether or not he'd noticed this too. When he glanced across at Rut he saw that, undoubtedly, he had also taken note of the development.

Lou stole another glance back to the front of the cart. The guards were still dealing with the elderly lady, attempting to console her, putting out the fire with a combination of rags they'd snagged off the cart, while she stood there screaming at the top of her lungs and appearing to beat them back.

Lou looked to his side, to the door of the cart. It was only fastened with a slide-bolt. They'd taken no other measures to keep them from escaping. There were three armed guards, after all. And Lou guessed that the driver was probably packing something —at the very least a dagger.

It would have been so simple if it hadn't been for their shackles.

The fire now out, Lou watched on as the guards up ahead attempted to move the elderly lady from the middle of the road, all three of them trying to get a hold on the sleeve of her robe, but somehow unable to cling on to the material.

Again, Lou glanced to that slide-bolt and, before he really knew what he was doing, he was leaning over and, with his bound hands, and flinging it back.

At the very periphery of his hearing, he heard that *snick* sound as the metal rattled back, and he watched the door swing wide open.

He glanced back and saw that both Sully and Rut were with him now. The two of them shuffling themselves sideways, making their way out of the cart, while still keeping their focus on the guards up ahead, checking over their progress with the elderly woman.

Lou shuffled over to the edge of the cart, slid his legs round, and perched on the ledge, ready to drop.

It was now or never. This was the point of no return.

For the flash of a second the possible repercussions of what he was about to do struck him.

Imprisonment?

They were *already* imprisoned.

Flogging?

Perhaps.

Execution?

That was a distinct possibility.

And yet, he allowed his legs to swing back just a couple more times before allowing himself to drop, the links of the chains that held him clinking together as he landed on the cobblestones.

Getting away. They were getting away.

18

ON THE RUN IN ILSNARE

AS LOU TURNED the corner into a side alley, and got out of sight of the guards, he felt the wind hit his cheeks, blast away the moisture there. His heart jigged up in his throat and he felt almost smothered by the scents of spices and herbs thick in the air. He sank his teeth into his tongue and willed himself forwards, to go faster, to go harder. But it was almost impossible. He could only shuffle forwards in his chains.

Lou could hear the slap of Sully and Rut's footsteps behind him, as they pushed to keep up. A bit further off, he could hear shouting, back in the street. The guards surely had noticed that they'd gone. And Lou knew they'd have no chance of beating them on foot, they'd have to find somewhere to hide out, or else they'd be caught and punished.

He eyed an open door up ahead of them, and he glanced round briefly to check Sully and Rut were still there, following him. Then he lurched in through the doorway, almost stumbling over his feet as he crossed the threshold.

Inside the house, the air was cool. He could smell the scent of bread baking. He could almost taste the rich smell warm his tongue. He heard the others still out in the alley, their chains clinking away as they came. Then he heard a guard bark something out.

For them to stop. This was the end. They'd be caught now. And tortured. Or killed.

And it would be all Lou's fault. He had initiated their escape, got them into whole new worlds of trouble.

And then there was a large, hefty *slap* as the door slammed shut behind him.

Lou glanced round, hardly able to believe it.

The door must've caught on the wind.

He glared back at it, a good dozen or so steps away. He shuffled his way back across the floor of the house, feeling his chains tighten around his ankles, and hearing them scrape against the brickwork beneath his feet.

As he drew closer to the door, he saw that not only had the door slammed shut, but the bolt had slipped across it. It was a bulky iron bolt, at least as thick as his arm. But it had apparently slipped across with the force of the shutting door.

He drew closer to the door and then lurched forwards, seizing hold of the bolt with his chained wrists.

It wouldn't budge. Not even a little.

And as he stood there, trying to shift the bolt from its place, he heard one of either Sully or Rut outside, the tinkling of their chains against the cobblestones, draw up to the door and then begin to pound their fists against it.

The pounding got so loud, so hard, that Lou could see splits appearing in the wood. He watched a crack form as the base of the door, but it remained narrow and refused to expand any more.

Moments later and Lou heard the steady bootfall of the guards, their gruff voices . . . and then, to Lou's disgust, the *snap* and *snick* of whips on human flesh.

The banging on the door ceased. And out in the alley someone, Sully or Rut, groaned out in pain. Then he heard the tinkle of chains again as the guards grabbed them and set them back on their feet.

Lou ground his teeth and tried to yank the bolt back.

Still, nothing.

Realising he wasn't going to be able to move the bolt at all, he shoved his shoulder hard up against the door, and butted it several times over. The door only rocked a tiny bit on its hinges, but otherwise held firm.

Lou halted, feeling his chest rising and falling against his tunic, and he listened to the boots stamping their way away from the door, the tinkling of the chains too growing fainter. And he knew that they were leading Sully and Rut back to the cart.

This was it. This was the end. They were at the mercy of the Royal Guards of Ilsnare now, and Lou would be damned if he'd allow his . . . his *friends*, to be brutally punished, even *killed*, in his place.

He rocked back the few steps he could considering his chains, and then he rushed at the door for a final time.

He bounced right off the door and toppled to the ground. He landed with a *thud* and the *chink* of chains.

Pain flashed up his spine, and his vision blinked red.

He stared at the door, at its apparently flimsily cobbled together planks of wood, and he wondered at how it had held on so strong, without so much as a dent from his last attempt to burst through it.

And as he listened to the clanking of chains outside grow dim, before fading away entirely, he heard those familiar stamps of boots heading up to the door. And then the pounding of a fist, followed by the familiar, hoarse voice of one of the guards.

"Oi! You seen anyone pass 'long here?"

Lou felt his heart swell in his throat. He knew that he had to cry out, that he had to answer the guard, tell him that he was hiding out here. No way could he allow his friends to go alone up against whatever the Royal Guards had in mind for them.

He had to stand up alongside them.

Another series of pounding on the door followed. "You deaf, or what? Open the bloody door right now!"

All the nerves and muscles in Lou's body seemed to tingle. Lou sucked in a deep breath, and then readied himself to cry out. . . . But he couldn't. He couldn't so much as raise a gasp.

He had lost the ability to speak.

He tried again, breathing in even deeper this time. But, again, nothing came out. His lungs felt like a bellows someone had punched a hole in.

Against his conscious thought, his breathing got shallower and shallower. He snatched breaths as quick as he could. He tasted blood in his mouth, thickening his tongue, making it completely unwieldy.

His heart rapped faster and faster.

More pounding against the door. "I'll go get a damn battering ram if you don't let me in here right now, you hear me in there!"

Lou knew it was futile. It didn't really matter, though. As long as he lay here, stayed right where he was on the ground, then the guard would go get that battering ram of his, and he'd burst his way in.

He would find Lou right here.

And then, from somewhere off in the back of the house, he heard footsteps.

Lou jerked his head around, his eyes rounded and full now. He wondered whether the owner of the house had been sleeping, and had only now been stirred by the racket at their door.

And then another thought skittered over Lou's mind.

Perhaps the owner was armed.

Lou waited there, feeling his heart beat harder and harder, before the owner finally slipped into view.

The owner wore a brown cloak, the ones that the monks often wore. And then, as he watched the hem of the cloak sweep at the feet of the owner, it dawned over Lou that this was a hobblesman. No, looking at the stature, the way that form had stamped itself on Lou's mind, he knew that it was *the* hobblesman he'd seen before the cursed bears had come.

The hobblesman didn't seem to notice Lou at all, simply wandering over to the door.

Lou lay there, on the floor, prostrate, exhausted. His lungs tingling now as he felt the lack of air getting to him.

He needed to calm down.

He remembered once when he'd been out bringing in the yield one year and he'd watched a man of thirty or forty who'd been going hard, his shoulders rapidly rising as he swept the corn over, collapse over on his side and breathe himself to death. His red face, those puffed out cheeks, and his tunic soaked with sweat. How they'd all stood over him, knowing there was nothing they could do, still returned to Lou. He'd seen that red face often in his dreams.

His nightmares.

Lou couldn't be that man. He had so much at stake. He had to stand beside Rut and Sully. He had to find out what had happened to the remaining villagers of Endmere. He had to return to take care of Syre.

And he couldn't do any of that *dead*.

He breathed easier now, watching the back of the hobblesman as he, apparently with little effort at all, swiped back the bolt then brought the door open with a shrill *creak*.

Lou watched the guard appear in the doorway, determined not to look away, not even to blink. Sure they could take him, but he wouldn't give them the satisfaction of showing any fear. He was a skuller, and he was determined that, if it came to it, he'd die like one.

The guard blinked as he stared into the gloom. He had his fist drawn back, in mid-air, ready to come down pounding out another knock against the door. His lips were slightly parted, a bit surprised. And then, slowly, he brought his gaze into focus on the hobblesman.

Lou waited for the moment when the guard would look

beyond the hobblesman, look over his shoulder and into the house.

Right at him.

But, for the time being at least, he was concentrating on the hobblesman, the owner of the house.

The guard sneered lightly. "Been sleepin' or what, eh?"

The hobblesman spoke with that drawling, slightly frail tone that Lou remembered so vividly. It was his last memory before the cursed bears had shown up. "Yes," the hobblesman said. "I was sleeping."

Now the guard did look around, behind the hobblesman, into the house. And, Lou was certain, just for a second, that he met the guard's eye, straight on. But, instead of the guard barrelling forwards into the house, shoving the hobblesman out of the way to recapture Lou, he returned to look at the hobblesman.

A spark ran around Lou's veins, bouncing about, tickling him from the inside. And he knew that something was up, that the guard had looked right at him

... but he had done nothing.

Lou lay in his place, perplexed.

The guard was a little less sure now, too. It seemed like his logical brain was taking over from his animal one, the animal brain that seemed to take hold of all men who carried weapons. He seemed like he might be just a little reluctant about having over-stepped the mark with the owner of this house ... just an elderly man.

"Had some escapees," the guard said. "Could be that one of them slipped in here."

"No, sir, I really don't believe so. I keep that door bolted all through the day." The elderly man chuckled. "And from what I heard of your buckling of its hinges, the lock is very much secure and in place."

A slight frown passed over the guard's face, and Lou knew that the hobblesman making a slight about guard's strength wasn't any way to get him to leave sooner. The guard narrowed his eyes. "One of my prisoners was rapping against this door—crying out. They wanted to get inside. That makes me think that the other prisoner's inside. If you'll permit me to have a look and see?"

Lou's heart thumped louder and he felt all the muscles in his body draw tight. Now he felt worse. He knew that the elderly man would also get in trouble if the guard found Lou hiding there all along.

It would just be another thing on his conscience.

The elderly man hovered in the doorway for a moment, apparently deciding whether or not he might have the strength to see off this stranger attempting to get into his house. Then he took a decisive step back.

The guard sniffed and then stepped over the threshold.

The guard had thick haunches, and he wore a scimitar down at his side. It reminded Lou a little of Sully, the way that the guard constantly kept his fingertips touching the hilt of the scimitar, ready to draw it at a moment's notice.

As Lou lay there on the stone floor, feeling the coolness of the slabs against his skin, he felt his gut wrench tighter and all those smells of bread thicken in the air, so much so that they seemed to smother him. Still he couldn't call out to the guard—put an end to whatever game this elderly man was playing, this game that would get the elderly man into just as much trouble as Lou was already in.

The guard snorted as he stepped into the house. He glanced about. Looked into every crevice. Then he stepped forward again, his foot landing right between Lou's legs. And still, *somehow*, he didn't see Lou.

It seemed to Lou that he was invisible, or that the guard simply refused to see him.

Just as the guard took another step, ready to land his boot into the middle of Lou's groin, the elderly man snatched the guard by his forearm and steered him off in another direction. "Here," the elderly man said, "you should come and check round back. He might've gone hiding in the preserves I keep back there."

The guard withdrew his boot, brought it back down, and then, with a distinct and lingering gaze right at Lou, he went after the elderly man.

Again, Lou was certain the guard had seen him, and yet he'd done nothing. Hadn't he been sure that he'd seen Lou there? Was that the problem? If only Lou could've called out, raised the alarm about just where he was lying, perhaps attempted to bargain the salvation for the elderly man, pleaded with the guard for him not to punish him too for apparently hiding Lou there the whole time.

But Lou couldn't make so much as a peep.

Lou lay on the ground, listening to the elderly man escorting the guard about the house, speaking all the time, muttering things to him about prisoners, and how they were terrible people who needed punishment, and how he'd once had a nephew that he'd turned into the Royal Guards for stealing a strand of pearls.

Lou knew just what he was doing. That the old man was somehow attempting to convince this guard that he really had no business looking through the house—that the old man was on his, and the king's side. He held no stock in hiding fugitives. And yet Lou couldn't help wonder just why the old man was doing this for him. Why *was* this old man trying to look out for him?

. . . And what the hell had he done to this guard so that he couldn't see Lou lying right there in the middle of the entrance hall?

Lou counted the ticking of his heart as he listened in to the ongoing search, and then, after they'd been through the entire house, he heard the old man and the guard's footsteps sounding on the stairs as they made their way back down.

Lou tilted his head up to look at them, at the same time feeling that same lingering tingle that told him that he would be found out at any second, that they would both stare right down at him lying there.

But they didn't. They just kept walking. All the way to the front door. Neither of them paid Lou any mind whatsoever.

Lou watched on as the door slipped open and then slammed shut again, behind the guard.

His heart hammered in his throat as he watched the old man —the hobblesman—turn to look at him. Although he couldn't make out the man's face from the shadow of the hooded cloak he wore, Lou was certain that he wore a wry smile.

"Now," the old man said. "That wasn't so hard, was it?"

19

TAKING REFUGE

LOU SAT UP in his bed, feeling the silk sheets drawn right up to his chin. The sun shone in through the windows warming him there. He could smell the sweet scent of freshly baked bread coming from downstairs, the slight *clank* of pots and pans. He envisioned the old man down there, busy in his kitchen, getting breakfast ready. He was getting breakfast ready for Lou, he knew that. But why? What had happened? How had he woken up here in this bedroom?

He stared about the bedroom. Bookshelves lined every wall, stretched right up to the plaster ceiling. The books were all battered, leather-covered hardbacks. The types that his ma had kept in the hall, the ones she'd used for reference whenever she had an especially difficult case, someone who'd come down with a fever, or cut their foot on a scythe, and it'd started to go black. And, Lou thought to himself, just like that book which Syre kept with her.

The one called *A Practical Understanding of Dark Magic.*

His skin prickled into goose bumps just thinking about that book, and the ones that surrounded him now. He couldn't make out the spines of them, the golden lettering was so faded and his vision was still a little blurry from sleep.

He thought back to his final memory. Lying on the floor, in the front hall of the house . . . this house, the one that he was sitting in right now. And he thought about the guard, how the guard had stumbled about looking for him, and how he couldn't find him. Then the old man turning on him, muttering something or other. Then he'd woken up.

Here.

He glanced over to the chair beside him, and saw his skuller's uniform draped over it, the boots standing underneath it. The old man had undressed him and put him to bed. That seemed quite a great deal for a frail-looking old man to do.

He tossed off the sheet and headed over to the chair. He examined his uniform, held it in his hands and looked over it. It smelled freshly washed. There was no hint of the sweat and dust that should've clung to it.

But, Lou noted, it was also bone-dry.

Downstairs, a pan clanked.

A shiver ran up Lou's spine, and he spun to look to the closed bedroom door. His mind whirled back to his friends, to Sully and Rut. He had to find out just where they'd been taken. He couldn't afford to waste too much time. And the others too.

Syre.

But if he left now what chance would he have? He had no weapons, and little training. He was barely worth being called a skuller. In fact, he was only known as a rookie. He wouldn't hold up to the grand might of the Royal Guards.

No, it was better that he took his time, that he worked out just what was going on, why the Royal Guards had imprisoned all of them. Then he could think about how he might move forwards. How he might manage to free them. How he might manage to free Syre.

He tugged on his skuller's tunic, and prodded his legs through the pair of trousers. He felt better in those clean clothes, in those skuller's clothes. It was like he had some sense of identity even here in this unfamiliar city.

The Crystal City.

He stuck his feet into his boots, noticing that they were both polished up bright and shiny. When he gave them a sniff, he again came away with none of that sweaty stench that had seemed to follow them all around, as they'd wandered about the plains looking for somewhere safe for them to go.

He made for the door, waited there a couple of seconds, still listening to the kitchen sounds down below, then he turned the handle and shuffled down the stairs, keeping to the rug down the middle to keep his footsteps silent.

His plan now was to get out there, back into the city, perhaps he could find the answers he needed out there. He just needed to disappear for a while, to have some time to think.

Whatever had happened the day before, he knew that he had to get far away from this elderly man—this hobblesman. He had no intention of drawing the man into all this. It was a lot of trouble for him to get himself wrapped up in. No, now it was time for Lou to take the initiative, to start showing some of those aspects which would see him qualified as a fully-fledged skuller.

Lou reached the bottom step and stared intently at the kitchen door. Those smells of freshly baked bread were pretty much over-whelming now. He felt his stomach groan with hunger and he pressed his hand to it, trying to stop it making a sound. Then he shifted off, rounding the staircase and beat a retreat for the front door.

Just as he laid his hand on the sliding bolt there, he heard, over his shoulder, drifting along the corridor from the kitchen, "Your mother never teach you manners?"

Lou's hand froze on the bolt.

The hobblesman apparently had great hearing to go with whatever it was he'd shown the day before.

Lou glanced back over his shoulder, half-expecting to see the hobblesman standing there in the doorway. But there was no one there.

He kept up his hold on the bolt a few moments longer, then sighed to himself. He knew that he would be doomed if he headed out into the city. Most likely Maun Fleeter would have the whole of the Royals Guards out searching for him.

Lou glanced down at his tunic, and realised he had been about to step out into that city still wearing his skuller's uniform. He wouldn't have been surprised if someone hadn't run to the Royal Guards the second he stepped out the door.

"Well, staying for breakfast, or what?" the hobblesman said.

Lou stood stiff for several seconds longer, then he made up his mind.

Who was he kidding? He would get eaten alive in this city. He needed all the help he could get. And although whatever had happened the day before had been deeply strange, he had no reason to distrust this hobblesman.

After all, hadn't the hobblesman warned him about the impending cursed bears? If the hobblesman hadn't told him then mightn't those bears have just overrun the camp, killed everyone?

He stepped back from the door, and then ventured back through the house, to the kitchen.

Those smells of warm bread just smothered all other senses from Lou's brain when he stepped over the hearth and into the kitchen. He stood there, just feeling those smells wash right over him, strip away any other tastes that might've been lingering on his tongue. Then he looked about the kitchen, to the stove, to the bubbling pot there, and then to hobblesman standing at a clay oven, over in the corner of the room. He still wore the cloak, his face hidden in shadow, and Lou couldn't help but feel extremely uneasy about not being able to see his host's face.

"Well, take a seat, then," the hobblesman said, reaching into the oven and removing those piping-hot bread rolls, the most delicious bread rolls Lou had ever seen.

His stomach now grumbling all over, Lou took his seat at the kitchen table, drawing up one of the rickety wooden chairs before taking a seat. As he sat, he noted that the stiff, hard wood beneath his bottom was a real change from that feather mattress he'd slept on the night before.

He watched the hobblesman working the pot on the stove, and then producing some butter from a cupboard that creaked on its hinges as he opened it.

Lou felt a shred of confidence spark into life inside him. "Don't you think it's a little dangerous to cook in that cloak?"

The hobblesman cut the bread rolls in two and smothered butter onto them. The butter melted the instant it touched the warmed bread, and that creamy smell clawed through the air, tantalising Lou's nostrils. As if he hadn't heard Lou's question at all, or perhaps he was ignoring it, the hobblesman continued on his way, getting everything ready.

From the pot he produced a ream of sausages, all of them shrugging off condensation into the air. He set everything down on a plate and brought it over to Lou, setting it before him, then standing back, face still completely obscured, waiting for Lou to start.

Lou felt the hung pangs all over his body. But he still couldn't quite bring himself to start. Not with the hobblesman staring at him like that. And he had so many questions on his mind. So many matters of urgency. "Why *do* you wear that cloak?" Lou asked again, realising that his insistence was somewhat impertinent.

The hobblesman remained silent. "Eat your breakfast," he said, turning away. "We'll talk about that after."

Lou did scoff the whole breakfast down, hardly pausing to chew. He guessed that all the marching they'd done over the past few days, and all the stress thrown into it had taken its toll on his body.

Now he felt much fresher, he thought, owing to his decent night's sleep, and with a hearty breakfast inside him it was like he could take on the whole of the Royal Guards single-handed.

Or something like that.

He knew that he had to be patient, that he had to find out more before he rushed into his solution blind.

At some point while Lou was gorging himself on the sausages, the hobblesman had taken up the chair opposite. He didn't eat, though. He just sat there, watching, from beneath that hood of his. Lou couldn't shake the feeling that he was being stared at by death himself. Why wouldn't the hobblesman show his face?

Lou stared at his empty plate before him, and he knew that now was the time. He looked into the hobblesman's face, or as much as he could guess where his face was, considering the hood, and said, "Yesterday. What did you do? Why didn't they find me?"

The hobblesman remained still, silent for several moments. Then he said, "It was a simple mind charm. It's not so difficult to convince people that, really, they haven't seen anything at all."

Lou felt his heart chill, and his chest tighten. So this was magic. Whoever this . . . this hobblesman was, he was a magical being. Or so it seemed. "And back at Gwindermere? You . . . you . . . ."

"Yes," the hobblesman replied, "I *disappeared* there too. Which is to say that I convinced you that I wasn't there at all."

Lou thought to himself for a long time, trying to piece this together in his mind. Of course he'd heard of magic, everyone heard rumours about it. But, at the same time, it was the stuff of legends. Oh sure, he knew that Ma had her medicines, all those things which dabbled in magic . . . *white* magic. This, though, hearing this first hand. It was something different altogether.

Lou broke from his daze, reminding himself of just what he was supposed to be worried about, what it was his duty to do . . . *who* it was his duty to save. "The others, they're . . . they're—"

"They're imprisoned now, I'm afraid. The Royal Guards have them."

Lou shut his mouth, and waited for more explanation. It seemed like this hobblesman knew just what he was going to say right before he said it. When the hobblesman wasn't forthcoming with anything further, Lou decided to keep asking his dumb questions. "And what can I do to get them back?" he said.

"Ah, well, that's a very good question."

"And what's the answer?"

"If you ever want to see them again—*any* of them—then you'll need to stay very close to me. Very close indeed."

"Fine," Lou said, feeling his throat throbbing, his voice wavering slightly. "Whatever you say. I've just got to get them back. That's all."

"You're a skuller, I can tell from your uniform. I noticed when we met one another back at Gwindermere." The hobblesman paused, as if he'd heard something outside, in the street. It was impossible to know, not being able to see his face. Then, after another moment, he continued, as if nothing had happened at all. "Tell me, how long have you served as a skuller?"

Lou half-snorted a laugh. "Couldn't you tell me that?" Then, thinking that this hobblesman, this . . . *whatever* he was, had taken him into his home, protected him from the Royal Guards, fed him breakfast, and so he owed him a straight answer. "Three days," he said, before adding, "I think."

It had been such a bleary period of time that all the hours had seemed to blur together. It was hard to believe that so little time had passed, in fact. To think that three days ago he had been bringing in the yield, thinking that he would have his winter's supplement in his hand, just like always, and that he would get his family through another winter alive.

"And what about your abilities? How's your skill with a sword, a bow and arrow," the hobblesman paused before adding, "a crossbow?"

"Didn't you see me fighting the bears?"

This time the hobblesman snuck in a wry chuckle. It sounded bitter, and on edge in the otherwise warm and pleasant-smelling kitchen. "Yes," the hobblesman said. "It seems like you're at least a fast learner. Once you've learned something it stays learned. I'll give you that."

Lou stared into the gloom of that hood, trying to make out a feature, anything there.

But . . . nothing.

Whenever he was sure that he'd made out the slightest of forms, a hooked nose, or the twinkle of an eyeball, he lost it again.

"But no worry," the hobblesman continued, "we can work on it all. It will take us some time but as long as you're patient then we'll get there. I promise you."

Lou thought hard, trying to get himself back onto some kind of level-pegging with the hobblesman. He didn't like it when people insulted his intelligence, or made him out to be naïve.

Sure, he knew next to nothing about magic, but that didn't mean that he couldn't pick it up. Or that there were things that others knew nothing about. He was sure he could teach just about anyone in the world about how to bring the yield in.

When Lou spoke again, his tone was sharp. "And if you're so strong why don't you go after the Royal Guards yourself?"

This rendered the hobblesman silent again.

The only sound in the kitchen was the slight click of the fire at the stove as the coals shuffled about, burning themselves down.

Lou caught a hint of smoke in the air and it was bitter compared with the sweetness of the butter on his tongue. He reached and clasped hold of one of the table legs, felt the sure grain of the wood.

He remembered that when he'd been a boy his pa had carved him a horse, sanded it down, and he'd kept it by his bed . . . well, till the whole of Endmere had burned right down to the ground.

Now it was cinders.

But when he had been a boy, and he'd wake from a bad dream, he'd always reach out for that horse, and he'd stroke its polished form, and then feel for those familiar rough bits. Those rough bits reminded him of the table leg he touched now.

The hobblesman seemed lost in thought, and then, all at once, he broke out of it. "The question is, if you truly wish to save your people then what other choice do you have?"

Lou dropped his stare to the table before him. He unclasped his fingers from the table leg, and fanned out his fingers there on the table, laid them flat against the surface. "Then will you at least tell me why you're helping me with this?"

"Ah," the hobblesman replied. "We all have our secrets."

20

THE ARMOURY

SOON AFTER that morning, Lou buried his curiosity. He had the horrible, sneaking feeling that the hobblesman might be able to listen in on just what he was thinking, so he decided his best course of action was simply to concentrate on whatever he had in front of him.

Later on that morning, his mouth still full of the buttery goodness, and those bread rolls and sausages congealing warmly in the pit of his stomach, the hobblesman showed him down to a trapdoor, concealed beneath a rug that he'd presumably not thought of showing off to the guard while he'd been searching the place for Lou.

The hobblesman threw the trapdoor back, and it landed with a wooden slap, and dust rose into the air, smothering Lou momentarily before he got over it. The dust reminded him of being out in the fields, that corn dust all around. That was just about the only familiar aspect of this situation to him right now.

Lou hesitated, eyed the ladder there, and then the gloom below. He looked to the hobblesman, realising that he was just going to have to trust him, that just like the hobblesman said, Lou really had no choice in the matter. If he wanted to save his people then he would have to do just what he said. Lou was the outsider here, the hobblesman was the local.

After another moment's hesitation, Lou stepped down the ladder, rung by rung, feeling the flimsy wood give way beneath his weight, but stop short of completely bowing in on itself. And, before he knew it, he stood in the basement, looking up to the hobblesman, coming down the ladder after him.

Lou tried to peel back the gloom with his eyes, but had no luck. He didn't dare so much as take a step forward into the darkness. When he held up his hand before his face, he saw nothing but obscurity.

The hobblesman thrashed some flints together and lit up a torch, or at least Lou thought he did, since he never saw the flints themselves, only the spark, and then the ensuing flame.

But, before he had time to really dwell on that at all, he watched as the glow of the torch illuminated the whole basement, sending the darkness off scurrying for the corners.

All around him, hanging from all the walls, were swords, scimitars, maces, crossbows, bows and arrows, and the odd dagger. The blades all gleamed in the torchlight, and Lou had to squint to stop his eyes stinging. He glanced back to the hobblesman, his face just as obscured as ever, and then stepped forward to examine the nearest sword.

Lou knew very little about swords. Like most working hands, he had nothing else to think about except conserving his energy for the next day. And as his pa had been a carpenter, not a blacksmith, he'd never really been around swords much. Come to think about it, even the blacksmith back in Endmere hadn't had more than a half dozen scattered about his workshop, and all blunted, gathering dust.

The only *real* swords Lou had ever seen had belonged to the skullers. And even then, those swords were nowhere near approaching the condition of the ones down here in the hobblesman's basement.

He looked over the sword before him, the biggest one in the whole place, which was to say the biggest sword he'd ever seen. The blade was twice the width of his arm, and the hilt looked like it might weigh more than he did. The edge looked razor-sharp, and it was free of nicks or scrapes. It was simply polished steel. He had never seen anything so beautiful.

The hobblesman laid a hand on Lou's shoulder.

A slight warmth emanated from beneath the man's fingertips. It was the first time the hobblesman had touched him, at least while Lou had been awake since he had no idea how he'd ended up out of his uniform and tucked up in bed the night before.

The hobblesman, however, didn't so much as flinch. In fact, he tightened his grasp. The warmth got hotter. "You might be better served with something smaller, I think."

Lou chanced a glance back, hoping this time to get a look at the hobblesman's face. But, too soon, the hobblesman had turned away from him. His hand leaving Lou's shoulder too as he went.

The whole notion of these weapons down here, the diminutive stature of the hobblesman, the obvious frailty and daintiness about the way he moved, was slightly ridiculous. But the man claimed he could help him get his people back, and Lou supposed that there was no option but to go along with all of this.

If Lou wanted the chance of *not* dying in the process, that was.

The hobblesman led him along the row of swords, the blades of which seemed to get stubbier, shorter, as they went on their way.

He paused at one of the smaller swords, slipped Lou a sidelong glance then said, beneath his breath, but loud enough that Lou could hear it, "I wonder," before stalking on a little further.

Intrigued, Lou followed him, seeing that he was leading him to where the daggers were.

He didn't look *that* scrawny did he?

The hobblesman stopped when he reached a particular dagger.

There didn't seem to be all much remarkable about the dagger, and Lou was lost as to why he'd brought him before it. He cast his eye over it again. Well, perhaps there *was* something remarkable about it.

To begin with, the handle of the dagger was wrapped in ragged cloth, and made it look somewhat untidy compared to the beautifully maintained other weapons. The edge, though, looked just as sharp as all the others.

But, apart from the rag around the handle, there was nothing that set it out, though Lou supposed that he'd have no trouble brandishing it.

The hobblesman slipped Lou a sidelong glance, then nodded to the dagger. "Go on," he said. "You take it."

Lou stood stiff in his place, a second or so, then he reached out for the handle, for those rags bundled round it. As he clasped his fingers round the handle, he felt a shiver pass right through him. He locked his teeth together, his heart tapped out double, then triple time. His whole mind seemed to shut down, and his vision grew dark around the edges.

But he held on.

And after a moment or so passed, he could just about stand the shuddering sensation passing through the handle, and taking hold of his whole body.

With the dagger in his hand, he looked to the hobblesman. "What ... what is this?" he said.

The hobblesman stared out at him from beneath his hood, those features still impossible to read, and the torch which he held in his hand, just to the side of his head, casting all the more shadow over him. "Put it back," he said.

As Lou examined the dagger he held in his hand, he saw that he'd only drawn it about an inch out of its bracket on the wall. It took him a moment or so to communicate just what he wanted to do to his fingers, and he watched, almost detached from his hand, as he let go of the dagger and it slipped back into place.

Again, Lou looked to the hobblesman, still wanting him to answer his question.

The hobblesman sidled on, heading back along the row of swords, looking just as determined as before. "That," he said, "is what's known as the Webbing Blade."

"What's it for?"

The hobblesman continued to peruse the swords up on the wall, apparently looking for something which might suit Lou. "It's a magical blade. *Ice* magic."

"And what does that mean?"

"It *means* that it's exceptionally effective—nothing short of a magical artefact. That blade will normally freeze the skin of any non-magical being. Kill them dead. One touch of even the handle, simply being around the Webbing Blade, has been known to send mortals into comas."

Lou felt his heart patter in his throat. He wondered if the hobblesman was telling the truth. If so, then he had every right to be furious. What did he think he was doing by putting him into extreme danger like that?

But Lou managed to keep a wrap on his emotions, enough to ask, in a rational voice, "So why didn't it kill me, or send me into a coma?"

"*Because* it appears that you have ice magic in your veins."

"Ice magic?"

"Yes."

Lou felt as if the hobblesman was talking down to a child, explaining adult stuff that he'd never be able to fully-comprehend. "And how did you know I had ice magic in my blood? How could you have been so sure that it wouldn't harm me?"

When the hobblesman spoke again, Lou was sure that he felt a slight smile in his voice. But, unable to see the man's face, he had no way of knowing for sure. "I like to think that I have a good intuition about people."

21

IN TRAINING

THE HOBBLESMAN picked out another cloak from within his wardrobe. It matched the one that he wore. He informed Lou that it might not be the wisest move for him to go out striding through the streets of Ilsnare in his skuller's uniform.

That would simply lead to his recapture.

The hobblesman fitted Lou out with a sword, a shield, and a crossbow, which he had him put on beneath his cloak.

Lou felt weighed down under the load of arms, and his nostrils were thick with the smell of highly polished steel and the leather of the straps.

When he walked, he could hear the blade of the sword scrubbing against its sheath, and his footsteps seemed to be twice as loud from all the weight he was carrying.

Before they left the hobblesman's house, the hobblesman gave Lou another few bread rolls to take on the journey.

But before they'd even reached the front hall of the house, Lou had devoured them all.

Their trip through the city was eerie for Lou. He couldn't help but glance round himself every couple of footsteps, sure that there would be a Royal Guard ready to grab him, to slap him into chains and drag him off . . . well, wherever they'd taken Sully and Rut, and the rest of the villagers.

Lou watched the hobblesman closely as they skittered through the market stalls, passed the tangy odour of fish hanging up, and the freshly baked, sugary-smelling buns.

As they wandered on past the soup kitchen, Lou was almost certain that his stomach was going to physically stop him, *force* him to buy a bowl. And he supposed that it was his force of will which dragged him onwards, which kept him going.

They proceeded on their way to the outer fringes of the city, and then out through the gates, manned by a pair of Royal Guards who looked much less interested than those that had been at the main gates when they'd come along Capital Road.

Still, the guards did approach them. One of them grunted something about identification papers, but the hobblesman simply reached into his robe and withdrew a small purse, which clinked with grung.

Coins.

And he handed it over into one of the guard's lazy hands. Then Lou and the hobblesman simply wandered on.

The hobblesman leaned back into Lou and muttered, under his breath, "This is the north-west entrance. If you'd really known what you were doing around Ilsnare, you never would've come in the south entrance. *That* was your mistake."

As they passed through those stone pillars, and the lazy-looking guards on either side, Lou felt his heart swelling up in his throat, and his blood pumping hard into his head.

They had been so naïve.

If only he'd opened his eyes, spoken more in the fields with the other working hands, then maybe they might've avoided getting into trouble. And yet, surely Sully should've known? Hadn't he said that he had visited Ilsnare before, or had he said that he'd been born here? Lou couldn't really remember. But he swore that he'd never make the same mistake again.

They emerged out on the plains, and Lou heard the birdsong in the air, sharp in his ears, and he felt the softness of the earth beneath his feet. This was so different from the hard road they'd trodden for the past few days. And he felt his heart lighten a little to be out of Ilsnare.

Getting out of the city was like having a noose loosened from his neck.

It was still around midmorning, so the sunlight still made the dew on the long grass glisten, and Lou could smell the dampness in the air—that freshness he always remembered from his early-morning journeys out to the fields.

Feeling his load growing heavy again, he shrugged his shoulders, tried to loosen them up, and he felt his weapons moving against his body. Already he could feel them imprinting themselves on his skin, and he guessed that if he carried them for long enough he would get used enough to their load so as never to notice.

That was how it had been out in the fields, with the ploughs, or with his scythe, soon enough his hands got calloused enough that the tools just seemed to fit there, become a part of him. And now he was a skuller, he guessed that his sword and his crossbow, let alone the shield, which skullers didn't carry, would become his tools of the trade.

The hobblesman walked quickly, much quicker than the hobbling hobblesmen were noted for, and Lou was beginning to wonder how much of the hobblesmen's appearance was genuine, and how much was an act.

A ruse to go unnoticed.

This hobblesman, in any case, seemed much sprightlier, much more sharp-witted than any other he'd encountered.

When they'd climbed a hill, scrambling up a rock face, a forest emerged beyond them. It was darkened, even in the strengthening sunlight, and Lou could smell the fresh breeze blowing through it, bringing all those earthy smells along too. But they didn't go into the forest, because at this point the hobblesman simply turned and faced up to Lou.

"You can take your cloak off now," the hobblesman said.

Lou glanced round him. Off, in the distance, about a mile or so away, he saw Ilsnare stretching out for miles and miles in length. The wall stood in the foreground, that same pit-black he'd noticed earlier. The sun caught the glass rooftops, and sent some of them sparkling, just like the crystal that gave the city its nickname.

He shucked his cloak, letting it fall into a pile at his feet, and then he turned his attention to the hobblesman, waiting for his orders. Suddenly, inexplicably, he felt a rush of confidence, to bring up just what had been bothering him ever since they'd met. He stared into the darkness of that hood, still trying to make out the features there. But having no luck. "Aren't you going to take off *your* cloak?" Lou said.

The hobblesman only responded by reaching into his cloak and withdrawing his own sword. Lou hadn't even seen him putting it on, hiding it under his cloak, or had the hobblesman had that sword on him the whole time? Even when he'd led that Royal Guard about his house.

It seemed like everything about this hobblesman was a surprise.

But, before Lou could speculate any further, the hobblesman rushed for him, swinging his sword, the blade whistling through the air.

There was nothing half-hearted about the swing.

The hobblesman went right for Lou's neck, and if Lou hadn't ducked then the hobblesman would've clean taken his head off.

Lou did duck, though, falling down to his knees more out of instinct than anything else. Those same instincts, Lou supposed, that had kept him alive while they'd fought off the cursed bears.

The hobblesman came again, thrusting the sword down this time.

Lou barrelled over onto his side. He felt the dew on the long grass soak his tunic, moisten his skin beneath the material. His whole world seemed dominated by the stench of earth, and the light scent of steel.

The hobblesman stabbed down.

Lou rolled over once, twice, and then, realising he'd reached the edge of the hill, he stopped seeing that he could roll no longer. He glanced down, over the edge, to the drop below.

He saw the jagged rocks sticking out of the hill face that they'd just climbed. If he fell badly down that slope there would be no telling just what damage he would do himself.

A broken leg.

A broken neck.

It would put his hopes of recovering the others at grave peril.

Put his hopes of saving Syre at risk.

And so, with that on his mind, and the hobblesman looming above him, drawing the blade back, apparently for the killing stroke, Lou summoned his strength from somewhere—perhaps from those delicious bread rolls the hobblesman had fed him before they'd left the house—and he lurched back up, first into a crouch, and then back standing.

The hobblesman held his sword down by his side. That void beneath his hood expressionless like always. "You think that Herimyre'll give you a chance to draw your sword before he slices you up?"

"Herimyre?" Lou said, thinking that the name sounded familiar, but unable to place it. "Who's Herimyre?"

The hobblesman kept hold of his sword, gripped down by his thigh, and Lou knew that in a single, swift motion he could easily rush him again. "Herimyre is the Captain of the Royal Guards. He's the one who's holding your people. If you want to save them, then you'll need to go to him, *kill* him, to set them free."

Lou felt his mind get smudgy, and uneven. He tried to meet the hobblesman's eye but, of course, he had no chance of doing so.

The hobblesman only had a shadow for a face.

"How will I even get to him?"

"You don't worry about that," the hobblesman said. "I'll take care of that. I can get you into a room with him, get you alone with him, but you'll have to do the rest."

Lou stood there a long time, feeling his muscles knotting, his mind unravelling. He had only just become a skuller, and he had lost all the mentors he'd ever known.

First Murch, and then Sully and Rut.

The only person who could even get him anywhere close to fighting shape, he now saw, was the hobblesman standing before him.

And still the question as to why he had to fight at all still plagued his mind.

"If you can get me in the same room as him then why can't you be the one to kill Herimyre?"

The hobblesman remained silent for a long time, and Lou was certain that at any moment, a moment of the hobblesman's choosing, he would burst out from his static pose and strike Lou with the sword.

Not just strike him. But *kill* him.

And then the hobblesman spoke.

"Because," the hobblesman said, "Herimyre can smell magic. He's a mortal but when he was very young, a tiny boy, a mage once tried to kill him. And he's recognised it ever since. He has the means to *resist* it. If I'm even within the same breathing space as the man he'll smell me coming, and he'll run me through with his blade faster than you can imagine."

"And what makes you think that I'd be able to kill him? Just like you've seen, I can hardly wield a sword, I just haven't had any practice."

Again, when the hobblesman spoke, that smile seemed to lift

the tone of his voice. "Because you have magical blood. But you don't practise magic. He won't smell you coming. And, what's more, it's *ice* magic that's in you blood."

"And what does that mean?"

"That you can get close enough to kill him with the Webbing Blade."

They passed the rest of the afternoon working on their sword-play, and Lou was sure that he was getting worse, although the hobblesman complimented him many times over.

Lou had to admit that he had lost those shakes he'd had before, whenever he'd taken hold of the hilt of a sword. Now he could clasp it firmly, and tightly without trouble.

After finishing up a final sparring session, and with the sun setting on the day, Lou collapsed over onto his back, feeling the sweat on his face, and the cool evening breeze blowing back his hair. He turned to look at the hobblesman, who was still on his feet, apparently unfatigued by the session, and replacing the sword back inside his cloak.

Lou took several deep breaths and then found his voice. "If you're so sure about getting me into the same room with Herimyre, getting close enough to stick him with the Webbing Blade, then what's all the point of the sword practice?"

Just as with his usual tricks, the hobblesman stayed silent for a long while, considering the question.

Lou had already come to recognise that gesture as a kind of holding back of information, and it made him feel like a school child—like the country bumpkin that he really was underneath. It was like the hobblesman was afraid of ladling burdensome knowledge on his shoulders, like if Lou knew too much he might not be able to carry out his role.

An ant's role.

The hobblesman turned his back to Lou, and looked off into the trees of the forest. The sun was drawing down over his shoulders as he looked off there, and his words were somewhat muffled, for the first time a little unsure. "When you've taken care of Herimyre, I want to build an army. An army that will set everything right again."

He turned back and glanced over his shoulder and, for just a micro-second, Lou was certain that he saw a twinkle in his eye. "These lands are diseased, *cursed*, and it must be set right.

"But before that can happen, traitors must be dispensed with, the laws must be re-written, and a new ruler must be put in place."

Lou scoured his brains, trying to get straight exactly what it was that the hobblesman was saying. But he came up with only one conclusion. "You want to depose the king?"

Still turned to face Lou, the hobblesman gave him a gentle, doleful nod.

And Lou felt his cheeks getting caught in the chill of the wind. He felt his chest tighten and his throat stick.

What could he possibly say to that? How *could* he say anything to that?

Lou turned his head to look back at Ilsnare. He saw that the mist, that mysterious *cursed* mist was descending over it. They had waited too long, stayed out here for too long a time. They hadn't heeded the warning of the setting sun and fled back to the city. They would be out on the plains, at night.

Again.

Then, in the near distance, Lou heard the stirring of leaves. At first he was sure it was the wind, moving the branches, sending them creaking and groaning. And then, above their heads, coming at them like a dark cloud, he saw birds.

Thousands of them.

Crows.

Cursed crows.

22

CROWS

THE HOBBLESMAN turned round quickly, and dropped onto his front, just as the first crows beat their wings overhead. Their claws swooped down, trying to snatch hold of skin.

Lou felt his heart throbbing in his mouth, and a great chill pass over his whole body. He reached for his crossbow, still strapped to his back, and, moving quickly, he slipped a bolt into the mechanism.

Even as he stared along the sight he knew that there were too many of them.

Far too many of them.

But, still, he fired off bolts into the flock of crows, more of a cloud since it was so thick, and watched on as a handful of coal-black, feathered bodies dropped from the air and landed in the thick grass.

Lou looked to the hobblesman, saw that he'd drawn his own crossbow from his cloak. And he was peppering the crows with the bolts from it. The crows continued to hang back, in mid-air, not seeming to want to attack as one.

Yet.

With that thought in his mind, Lou saw the whole flock of them dive right down, come with their beaks sticking out, and their claws jutting towards them. There was nothing to do but throw himself down flat on the ground and cover the back of his head with his hands.

He felt their needle-sharp claws prickle his arms. He felt their beaks jab away at his skin. And he felt the steady throb of blood leaking out of his skin. More of them descended on him.

More and more.

There was a weight to them now. All of them on his body. All of them piercing his skin with their beaks and claws. Red flashes of pain flickered across his vision.

Thinking back on it, Lou wasn't all that sure when he first felt the warmth.

All he knew was that one minute he was being pecked to death, feeling the blood throbbing out of him, his body beginning to give itself over to the intense pain, his brain about to shut down. And, the next minute, he felt an overwhelming heat. Like that of a summer's day in the fields.

He cast his mind back to the day when they'd brought in the yield, and it played out on his mind. Once more he could taste that corn dust on his tongue, sticking to his sweaty exposed flesh, and he could smell that warmth all rising around him, like a blanket left by the fire.

And then he heard a sudden and distinct, *whooosh!*

Lou kept his face pressed into the earth the whole time. The mud was cool before, but it rapidly began to warm. And at first it was unpleasant.

And then *searing* hot.

Only when he tore his face away from the ground did he realise that the crows were gone. That they no longer lay over him. And his next observation was the roaring jet of flame which seemed to blast over the whole of the plains. Which blasted a couple of inches above him.

The flame filled his entire vision.

At first he thought he might be dead, that he was seeing the sun, that he'd got himself lost in the sun on his way to heaven, and then he watched as the light faded, just as quickly as it had come.

And then, all at once, the light dissipated. Completely extinguished itself.

All he saw was the hobblesman standing there, arm outstretched, those slender fingers sticking out from the darkness of his sleeve.

And the slight glow of his hand.

Lou felt a gentle layer of dust on him. It took him a moment to realise, when he brushed his hand across his cheek, that it was ashes.

The crows.

The hobblesman had turned them to cinders.

He had saved Lou from certain death.

Before Lou got the chance to piece his wits back together, to make some sort of sense of what he'd just witnessed, he noticed the hobblesman already making his way off down the hill, heading back across the plains for the north-west entrance to Ilsnare.

Lou stumbled up to his feet, slipping twice as he did so. He pulled his cloak back on, over his head to cover his skuller's uniform, and, just as he set off in pursuit of the hobblesman, he remembered his crossbow. He stooped to pick it up and shouldered it before jogging after the hobblesman.

The hobblesman proceeded at a steady march, gaze fixed ahead, not noticing Lou as he sidled up alongside him, panting away, mind aflare with wonder at how the hobblesman had dealt with the crows. "How . . . how," Lou began, but already knowing his question would be in vain. "How did you do that?"

The hobblesman just strode on, paying no attention to Lou, and Lou, more than once, glanced over his shoulder, convincing himself that a fresh batch of crows might be ready to rise from those trees, and to attack them again.

Though why should it trouble Lou, considering that the hobblesman could, apparently, turn them to ashes with flames from his hands?

When they got to the north-west entrance to Ilsnare, the same two Royal Guards stood there. The hobblesman made to hustle his way past them, when one of them said, in a gruff, thick voice, "Wait there a moment, will ya?"

Lou glanced to the guard who'd spoken.

To him all the Royal Guards looked much alike. They all wore that same pale grey uniform, and were bulky, with big muscles, their fists always tight around the handles of the spears or scimitars they carried.

This particular guard was larger than average. Not only was he broad, muscular, he wore a mean expression. He towered over the two of them by at least a head and shoulders.

Perhaps, two sets of head and shoulders in comparison with the hobblesman.

The guard had pin-prick eyes, as if, as an after thought, his creator had jabbed them into his lubbering, thick face. "Let me see your face," the guard said to the hobblesman.

Lou felt his body stiffen and he watched on to see what would happen.

The hobblesman just stayed still, not moving an inch.

Not looking to either obey or disobey the man.

The guard straightened his expression, any hint of joviality that had been there before was replaced by pure, unadulterated meanness. "You deaf?"

Still, the hobblesman remained where he was.

Lou wondered if the guards were going to ask him to remove his hood, too. But as he stood back from them, he saw that they only seemed interested in the hobblesman.

"Saw that fire out on the hillside, did ya?" the guard said, stooping over the hobblesman, bringing his face close to his hooded face.

No reply from the hobblesman.

"Funny that such a powerful fire went out so quick."

This time the hobblesman did speak back. "Maybe you were just seeing things. I didn't see any fire—not out there."

The guard snorted a dry laugh then glanced over to his companion. "That don't sound likely to me. Me and Gonrick here, we're picked to man the walls because we've got good eye-sight, you see? We've gotta report into the boss anything suspicious, like."

"And you don't think me palming you those grung earlier was suspicious? Do you think your boss would enjoy hearing about that?"

The guard broke out into a smile.

Lou saw that his teeth had a black-green coating, and that his tongue had turned a sallow shade. His breath reeked of onions from the broth he'd apparently recently ingested.

"Nah, that's all part of the job, that is," the guard said. "Boss knows how it is. He's on a salary just like the rest of us, knows that sometimes a man's gotta take just a little more to help feed his family." His smile slipped from his lips entirely. "A *fire* mage, though. That'd be a whole different matter. If there's a fire mage about, then . . . well, he'd most likely want to hear about that."

Lou processed the development, tried to stack it into some sense in his mind. That was right. That was what he'd seen. That burst of fire, the way the hobblesman had incinerated those crows. Why hadn't he thought of labelling it that way? He supposed there just hadn't been time. He had been so thankful that the hobblesman had saved him, brought him back from the point of death.

"Nonsense," the hobblesman said. "If I was really a fire mage, don't you think I'd have set the two of you alight by now?"

The guard was now totally graven-faced. His face looked cold, and his eyes got shifty. Lou saw that he tightened his knuckles about his spear, and Lou readied himself mentally to draw his sword. "Maybe we put you in shackles and put you to the test, eh?" the guard said.

The hobblesman remained silent.

Lou looked from one guard to the other, and the guard's

companion—the one who hadn't yet spoken—stepped over to the first guard's side and mumbled something in his ear.

The two guards stared at Lou and the hobblesman for a long time, and then the first guard, with a flash of his eyes and his teeth gritted, said, "Right you are, stranger. But you'd better take care coming through here the next time. My pal here's got a good shot on him with the crossbow, and even fire mages aren't that smart when they've got a bolt sticking out their back."

The hobblesman waited, still refusing to reply.

The two guards, with a final glance between them, stepped aside and let them through, back into the city.

Back into Ilsnare.

On their walk back through the city, Lou processed everything that had occurred, sorted it in his mind, tried to get the facts straight.

And he *was* beginning to put the pieces together, but none too quickly, or too smartly. He had to bide his time, await his opportunity. He had no intention of raking up the hobblesman's fury yet again.

They arrived back to the hobblesman's house, and they removed their weapons.

Lou was a little loathed to part with his crossbow and sword, although he could take or leave the shield.

And he watched on with a slight heaviness in his heart as he watched the hobblesman lug all the equipment back down through the trapdoor, back down into the basement.

Lou took up his place at the kitchen table, and listened to the sounds of the hobblesman returning all the weapons to their racks. And then to the shuffling of the hobblesman's footsteps up the ladder, and then the *thud* of the trapdoor shutting behind him. He watched the doorway as the hobblesman appeared there.

His face still as steeped in shadow as ever.

There was no point in wasting any more time. Lou had to just bring it out. So he did. "You burned down my village, didn't you?"

Lou had no idea what he had expected from his question. Perhaps another storm of fire, of that intense heat. But the hobblesman just lingered in the doorway. Silent. Just as he'd acted with those guards at the north-west entrance.

"Well?" Lou said, feeling his heart lurch up to his throat, and a hot rage build in his stomach.

The hobblesman moved out from the doorway, crossed the kitchen, and stood at the stove. He busied himself with something or other there, a pot or pan, Lou couldn't see exactly what it was because the hobblesman had his back towards him. When the hobblesman replied, Lou could hardly hear the tone of his voice, let alone believe what tumbled out of his mouth. "It was necessary."

Lou felt the rage twist his stomach, and he wished for those weapons, for that sword. That guard had said that he would have had his friend shoot the hobblesman in the back with a crossbow next time he headed out onto the plains, and Lou felt that same anger rising in him.

He rose from his chair, sending its wooden legs scraping against the floor of the kitchen. He stared intently at the back of the hobblesman's neck, concealed by the cloak, and willed him to look round at him, for the first time to meet him eye to eye.

The hobblesman half turned his head, and his voice never rose above a mumble as he spoke. "Please, you've got to believe me. If there had been another—"

This time Lou lurched forward, and he grabbed the hobblesman from behind. Lou's hand found the hobblesman's throat right away, snatching hold of it beneath the rough fabric of his cloak. He touched his skin. He was caught off guard by how fragile the bones there were, how they felt like they might snap if he just used enough force. He gripped him tighter, harder, and felt the strength flowing through his fingers readily now.

The hobblesman groaned out, in pain.

That flow of strength continued to pass through Lou's fingers and, when he glanced down at his hand, he saw that all the blood had left it. That his hand had turned a dark-blue tone. He was so surprised at the change that he let go of the hobblesman, watched him stagger away, retreat out from the kitchen.

Although Lou's logical mind demanded that he go after the hobblesman, that he track him down and finish the job—the job that his parents', and all the other villagers', memories demanded, he could only stare at his hand.

The dark, bruise-blue colour there.

And it felt cold.

Detached from him.

He snapped from his daze, looked to the kitchen doorway, and wondered just what the hobblesman had done to him.

What this . . . this *freak*, had done to him.

He glanced back at his hand, seeing the normal colour beginning to return, and he pounded off into the house, taking the stairs three at a time, hardly able to take a breath, his anxiety to catch up with the hobblesman and bring him to justice was so strong.

When he arrived up on the second floor landing, he forced himself to breathe. To take those long, cleansing breaths that he needed to take to keep his mind sharp, and his actions swift.

He had never been this close to magic before, and now he was determined to keep his wits about him. He knew that his biggest fear was the unknown quantity surrounding it. But, if there was something he'd learned over the past few days, of becoming a skuller, it was that fear was all there was to it.

He just had to press himself forwards, get himself out of his comfort zone. That was how he would have his revenge.

And how he would eventually rescue the others from the Royal Guards.

He stalked along the landing, feeling the wooden planks, the floorboards, retreating slightly, groaning a little, beneath his step. He thought back to the trapdoor, considered bounding down there and seizing hold of a sword . . . or perhaps even that Webbing Blade if he could stand the chill it gave him, but he decided that he simply couldn't allow this mage to slip through his fingers.

The hobblesman had to die.

And die *now*.

He approached the only other room up here on the second floor, the one that he hadn't slept in, and the one inside which he supposed the hobblesman to be hiding, waiting, lurking, ready for him.

But Lou was determined that he would be harder, and faster.

Stronger.

As he drew closer, he pressed his back up against the wall, and strafed his way along it. He listened hard, trying to get some sound, to work out what the hobblesman might have planned for him. He could hear breathing, long and then shallow.

Snatched breaths.

And he hoped that he had mortally—or was it immortally?—injured the man. That would be easier. He wouldn't have to administer the killing stroke.

He arrived at the doorframe and stood there, getting himself under control. Calling upon all his strength to push himself forward. He clasped his eyes shut, muttered something to himself, and, on the backs of his eyelids, he was sure that he saw his ma and pa's faces there, their eyes shining, smiling back at him from their place in the ever after. And, just like that, he burst into the room.

The first thing that stopped him in his tracks was the fact that the hobblesman had his hood draped down, head uncovered.

And the next was that long, unfurled blanket of flame-red hair.

Those fragile *feminine* features.

23

A HOBBLESMAN NO LONGER

ALL OF A SUDDEN, Lou felt very cold.

It felt like his body was floating away from him.

He was aware of the rub of his tunic on his stomach, of the residual chill on his fingertips, and of the gentle warmth in this room—certainly not coming from the sun since it had set long ago.

And he felt light as he took a step forwards, moving closer to the girl . . . the *woman*, that knelt down with her back towards him, the cloak still clinging to her frame.

She didn't turn round, and he took in that hair one more time.

It truly was like staring into a scarlet pit of a long-burning wood fire. That hair reminded him of the middle of winter, when he'd brought in the first sack of wood with his winter's supplement, and the looks on his parents' faces, the healthy red glow that would appear in their cheeks as they warmed themselves round the fire.

And now they were dead.

And this ... this, fire mage had done it to them.

And yet the anger seemed to have dissipated, to have diluted into Lou's bloodstream. He couldn't help but observe this woman before him, that hint of pearl-smooth skin he could see of her face in profile.

He simply couldn't get over the delicacy that seemed to linger over the whole of her, to make her seem vulnerable ... impossible of inflicting harm.

But she had.

She had inflicted *terrible* harm, on everyone Lou had ever known.

Murdered his parents.

She continued to face away from him as he approached. His brain told him that this was his opportunity, that he would never get another one like it again. That he had to finish off what he'd started. That he had to break that flimsy, slight neck of hers. Crunch those delicate bones in his grasp.

But he just couldn't bring himself to do it.

He couldn't bring himself to do it because, he knew, deep down, that he wasn't a murderer. This wasn't a cursed animal he was dealing with. This was a being of flesh and blood, just like him. And now that he'd ridden out the first flush of fury, he knew that he would never be stricken enough to do it.

She kept her head tilted down, staring into her lap.

Lou caught sight of her face in a mirror placed across the room. He stopped in his tracks, still about four or five steps from her, and stared at her reflection.

Her face was just as delicate as the back of her neck, and he saw, through her half-closed lids, that she had emerald-green eyes, bright and shined-up. Her skin reminded him of snowflakes, the way they settled together, and her nose was thin and a little pointed. He waited there, holding his breath, seeing if she was going to cry. He anticipated that single, snaking tear winding its way down her cheek. But that tear never came.

But she did speak.

"Please, make it quick," she said. "You're just as entitled to your revenge as I am to mine."

Lou stood there, still staring at that dainty face of hers. And he found himself wondering where that impossible strength of hers had come from, how she'd summoned up enough force to wield that sword, and to instil fear in him.

He waited for her to meet his eye, but she never did.

She just continued to stare down at her upturned hands in her lap, as if she was merely sitting here, in her room, on her own.

And his eyes wandered across her image in the mirror, down to her throat. He saw, right there, on her Adam's apple, she had a bluish welt. It took him aback as he realised that was the place where he'd touched her. And then he saw that it wasn't her who'd attacked him.

She hadn't done this to his hand.

It was *his* hand that had hurt *her*.

To confirm his suspicions, he looked at his hand, saw that it had returned to its normal skin tone, that slightly worn, leathery texture. There was no trace of the bluish colour that had been there before.

And then, just like that, those emerald eyes sought him out, met his. A faint smile traced her lips. "You could kill me so easily, if you wanted."

Lou couldn't think of how to answer, so he just stood there, feeling stiff as ever.

"That ice magic in your blood, just a touch of your bare skin on mine and you can take my life away." Her eyes searched his. "If you're going to do it, then do it quickly.

"Please.

"I've suffered enough."

Lou felt a faint flush of his anger from before, but it was nothing like the same intensity. Not enough to push him to kill, in any case. "And what about my people? All those innocent villagers? My ... my ma and pa?"

She continued to meet his eye, as she replied. "I'm sorry, but that was the only way. There couldn't have been another method that would've worked." She swallowed then said, again, "I'm sorry."

Lou felt that hum of fury inside him, and he felt his fingers curling up into tightly balled fists. He felt the sharp sensation of his fingernails burrowing into his palms.

He breathed in the room, getting a strong scent of cinnamon. Her smell. The one which she had kept so well smothered down, managed to make neutral, to keep up her disguise as a hobblesman.

"*Why?*" Lou repeated, feeling his throat scratchy and dry.

She looked away from him for a moment, glanced out the window into the darkness, to the flickering glow of the streetlights. And then, with a jerk of her head, she looked back to him. "Because, like it or not, there must be a war."

Lou felt his blood prickle in his veins, his heart squeeze blood harder. "What war?"

"Between the king and the people of the land. It's time to make a change. And for that we'll need an army . . ."

"And so the way you go about that is to burn down half the villages north of Ilsnare?!"

She pursed her lips, slipping into that same pensive silence she used in her hobblesman persona, then looked away again.

Lou thought back to his previous life, to his days as a working hand that were now long gone. Unless he could somehow manage to free his people and make a new life for them. Somewhere else. That fresh morning breeze, that click of the cartwheels as they rumbled their way along the beaten up tracks between the villages on their way to the fields.

That was all long gone now.

Lou shook his head. "We're not fighters. We're just ordinary people. And as for this *war*, what makes you think you have the right to even *believe* that's true? Who are you to say that we need anything changing? Do we look so wretched and depressed with our lives that you had to take the decision that we needed help?" His throat stuck. "That you had to burn down our homes?"

She stayed quite still.

"Well?" Lou said, feeling his rage bubbling back to the surface. His knuckles ached now that he curled his fingers so tight into his palm.

She met his stare with those brilliant, emerald eyes. "Burning down your homes was the only way for me to build an army, the only chance I had to flush out all the tough ones—the ones that could serve me as warriors. That might be able . . . be able to avert the larger war that's coming."

"And what *war's* that exactly?"

She parted her lips, widened her eyes and then shook her head, looking away again.

"Tell me," Lou said, gritting his teeth, and tasting blood in his mouth, his teeth pinching the inside of his cheek.

"You wouldn't believe me."

Lou let out a long, hard exhale, and then stared out the window, back into the darkened street.

Outside he could hear the *clop* of horse hooves, and, a little further in the distance, the echoing call of a vender, trying to sell some fabric or other. That cinnamon scent got stronger in the room, tickled his nostrils. His mouth watered a little. And then he stared back at her.

"If you won't tell me that, then will you at least tell me your name?"

Those emerald eyes of hers met his again, and Lou felt his heart give a little jig in his chest, his muscles tighten all over again. There was danger there. Extreme danger. Behind that beauty he saw relentlessness, a mean streak that had killed his ma and pa, burned those villages to the ground. He had to take care around her.

Extreme care.

"Hilda," she said, then, looking away from him, "but my father used to call me Hildie—I prefer Hildie."

Lou breathed in and out slowly, feeling the rage ebb out of him once again. He had to get himself calmed down, it would do no good for him to harm her. If she was telling the truth, that he would have to murder Herimyre to free his people, then he would need her help to get to him.

But first, he wanted to know. He wanted to know all of it.

And *right* now.

He turned to her. "Try and explain to me," he said. "I want to understand."

Hildie tilted her head down, stared at her upturned palms again, and Lou saw that delicate, cream flesh—it reminded him of the colour of the underside of a goose's belly. Like those geese they'd bring in over the winter when they'd celebrate Midwinter's Day.

And her skin looked just as smooth as those feathers.

"My father," Hildie began, "he was . . . he *is* a fire mage." She glanced up at him once more, those slightly curled, long crimson eyelashes of hers fluttering. "He was the one that cast the curse over the whole kingdom. He's the reason the mist descends at sunset, and at dawn."

"But, why?" Lou said.

She shook her head and stared at her reflection in the mirror. Looking there, into the mirror, Lou thought that he was somehow detached from the whole scene, like a simple shadow at Hildie's shoulder. A lurking presence there. He felt like he was almost floating outside of his body. "They captured his wife, my mother," Hildie said.

"Who did?"

She met his eye, and that hardness returned to her gaze, that *killing* hardness Lou was sure he'd seen there before. "The Royal Guards, *Herimyre*."

He saw now that there was a tiny sparkle to her eyes, and it took him another moment to realise that they were tears.

She continued. "It was while my father and mother were travelling along. I was only a child at the time, and we were hiding out in the forests, when they came across us. Herimyre was there with them . . . and . . . and, as my father told me later, he could simply *smell* magic on us, he knew just what we were.

"And my father was quick, he threw a . . . a flame bolt at the procession, killed them all before they could get us into the gaoler's cart. But Herimyre resisted. He drew his sword, and grabbed hold of my mother. He took her from us.

"There was nothing my father could do, he had to hold onto me, and he couldn't throw a fire bolt at Herimyre while he held my mother tight—he might easily have killed her too.

"Further up the road, coming down from Ilsnare, there was a procession of Royal Guards, dozens of them, all armed. And so all we could do, all my father could do, was retreat.

"I can still smell the burning fire in the air, it casting ash on my tongue, all those scorched corpses lying all around us, and Herimyre riding away with my mother as his prisoner."

She closed her eyes tight and, finally, Lou did see that single tear worm its way down her cheek. It settled on her chin and then dripped down into her hands clutched in her lap.

She took a deep breath, her shoulders rising and falling, then she glanced back over her shoulder at Lou. "My father bided his time, he waited a long while, wanting to get his plan perfect. And then he went to the palace, he went to Ilsnare, and he burgled his way in to see to the king there.

"He demanded that he let my mother go, but the king told him that she was already dead.

"My father barely escaped with his life. But he managed to cast the curse, to bring that deathly mist down upon Ilsnare every dawn and every dusk.

"And when my father returned, he brought me up on his own, out in the woods, on the very frontiers of the kingdom, he swore about how he would rouse a magical army, and bring it to bear on Ilsnare, put a stop to mortal rule once and for all."

She looked back down to her clasped hands, shaking her head. "Last week he left the house, and I know just where he's gone." She glanced back up at Lou. "He's gone to the Magical Council, to petition them. To bring the most powerful mages in the world here, to Ilsnare."

Lou stared back into her eyes. "And why's that any different from what you want to do? Didn't you say you wanted to depose the king?"

She gave him a wry smile. "You obviously don't know my father. Ma'reygar, the fire mage. If he manages to convince the Magical Council, they will enslave every non-magical being in the kingdom, and they will succeed."

She shook her head. "No, if we're to have any hope, any hope at all, then we must lead the people of the land to victory over Ilsnare—we *must* take over the kingdom for ourselves, instate a republic. Because when my father returns with his magical army, with all those mages he has managed to flush out of their various hiding places, *then* it shall be too late for reconciliation."

She breathed in deep again. "But if he sees that his daughter has done his work for him, along with the people of the land, that they've deposed of the king, of Herimyre, the ones that took away his wife, my mother, then perhaps it will cool his anger, and we can reach some agreement where all can live peacefully—one with the other, the magical and non-magical alike."

"How long till he returns?"

She shrugged. "A season cycle, years, decades. Who's to say? Maybe he shan't return at all. Maybe he'll fail to convince the Magical Council. That would be a mercy."

She met his eye again, and Lou felt another buzzing warmth in his chest. "But I wouldn't count on it."

Lou felt his mind getting away from him again, his rational thoughts telling him that this person, this *woman*, had killed his parents, had burned down his village.

She was responsible for him having lost his home forever.

But, at the same time, if he chose to believe her, if her father, this Ma'reygar, was really coming back, and that he would enslaved them all, then surely what she had done was only quicken the process. Still, he would never find a way to forgive her what she had done.

And why *should* he believe her?

Did he even have to?

After all, all he wanted was to get his people free, to get his friends Rut and Sully free, and his little sis too. That was his only goal. Wars, they were for the Royal Guards to fight. And he would ensure, once he got his people free, that he would get them far away from any chance of conscription in such a war, perhaps even over the border, into another kingdom.

But all that was a dream until he actually managed to get them free.

He would have to play along with Hildie's game.

Lou turned to face her, saw that blank expression of hers,

those slightly parted lips, and he couldn't help but think that she was beautiful, truly the most gorgeous woman he'd ever seen. And yet she was completely evil.

Worse than evil, ruthless.

But he would have no choice but to ally with her for the time being. Maybe later he could work out the subtleties of their arrangement, because he had no intention of getting wrapped up in a magical war.

All the same, they needed some sort of civility between the two of them, if they were to work together. And that started with them being on a level playing field in terms of what they knew.

"And the Webbing Blade?" Lou said. "What's the story with that?"

Hildie sighed. "My mother, she was an *ice* mage. That was her weapon. Throughout the land there's a legend, the legend of the Spider Warrior. An ice mage. The three magical artefacts once formed his armoury: The Webbing Blade, the Webbing Bow and the Webbing Cloak."

"And where are the others?"

"Who knows," she said. "But I often asked my father about it, where my mother got the Webbing Blade from, how she obtained it. He would never answer me. And so, I suppose, he never really knew. Most likely it was passed down from her father or mother, from my grandparents.

"The Webbing weapons are all extremely powerful magical artefacts. And combined, bringing them all together, will create the greatest strength granted to any ice mage."

"But you're a fire mage, so the Webbing Blade's no use to you?"

She smirked. "Yes, I can use the Webbing Blade, but I have to take care. If I don't use the wrapping round the handle then it can freeze my hand right off. And its power when I, or my father—another fire mage—wield it, is about the tenth of someone, say, like you."

"Like me?"

"Yes," she said. "You have ice magic in your blood." She narrowed her eyes. "Your mother, perhaps? Was she a medicine woman?"

Lou felt a glow pass through him, a stirring in his chest. "She was."

"There you have it."

She straightened her back and then, using her elbows, she rocked herself back up onto her feet. She padded over to the window and stared out through the glass, into the street. "Fire beats ice every time on a level playing field. Pure, unadulterated, brute force, nothing that can be done." She snuck a glance back at him. "And because my father was a fire mage, and my mother an ice mage, fire won out. And so that's who I am."

Lou felt a slight dip in his chest as he contemplate this. "So, what you're saying is that ice magic is just some sort of subservient form, compared to fire?"

"That might be one way to describe it, though each forms of magic have their own power. You, for example, wouldn't have survived that scorching fire storm I summoned to take care of those cursed crows if you hadn't had ice magic in your blood. Traditionally the ice mages are sleek, stealthy, hard to catch. They like to keep the shadows, hidden, till they leap out and slash your throat."

Lou felt that prickling sensation in his veins yet again, and he felt his mind flooding with all the details of the day, the sword fight, the crows beating down on them, and now, this, the fire mage who had been disguising herself as a hobblesman all along.

Hildie turned away from the window, made her way across her room, to the wardrobe she kept there. She opened the doors with a rusty creak of hinges. "Your mother did very well to keep herself hidden away for so long—to keep herself away from suspicion. Not many can manage it. Although, I suppose it *would* be an ice mage that would carry out something like that successfully. A fire mage would never manage it. We don't have the patience."

Lou continued to stare at her back, at those shoulders nestled beneath that brown cloak. He couldn't help wondering whether her skin was as fair on her shoulders as it was on her cheeks.

She glanced back from the wardrobe, from those garments all nestled inside there. "Help me find something, we don't have much time."

"Not much time for what?"

"To get to Ilsnare Palace before sun up."

24

ILSNARE PALACE

COMPARED WITH HOW he'd felt earlier on in the day, with his sword, shield and crossbow all nestled against his body, Lou felt almost naked beneath his cloak.

It was the same hobblesman's cloak he'd worn that day to go to training, but underneath it he now wore a beige tunic, and a pair of what could only be described as working-hand trousers. The only weapon he wore was the Webbing Blade, hanging from its sheath at his hip.

After they'd finished their heart-to-heart up in Hildie's bedroom, she'd brought him back down to the basement, back to her armoury, where she'd had him take hold of the Webbing Blade, at first only gripping it in his hand for a matter of seconds before releasing it.

Over the course of an hour, he'd increased the amount of time he held it, until he almost grew used to that biting chill which seemed to freeze the blood in his hand.

Now, as they strode along the shadows, the outskirts of the palace walls, he could feel his heart thumping against his tonsils and a thin layer of sweat break out at his lower back.

He kept his eyes locked onto the back of Hildie's cloak, watching it sweep the backs of her heels. He tripped a couple of times on the cobblestones, but kept himself upright. He felt that fury stirring inside him once more, but this time it wasn't directed at Hildie, but at Herimyre.

The man responsible for holding all his people, keeping them locked up.

But could he *kill* him? Really?

While he'd grown accustomed to the Webbing Blade so that he could now take the handle in his hand without the protection of the bandages, Hildie had explained that the Royal Guards, perhaps alerted by Herimyre's unusual sense for detecting the stir of magic, had become more careful with people arriving into Ilsnare, especially large groups.

Herimyre perhaps already knew that there was a war brewing on the horizon.

And that he would have to take care.

Hildie stole them in through a side door in the palace wall. She held her hands to the sturdy wooden door, and a steady orange glow passed from her palms and then incinerated the wood right before their eyes.

They walked through, into the palace gardens.

Lou wasn't quite sure exactly what he had expected, he supposed that he thought there might've been patrolling guards, something like that. At least someone up on the ramparts.

But here, in the darkness, the whole palace seemed deserted.

Back at her house, she'd told him that the palace gaol, where

Lou's people would be held while they were judged for witchcraft, was located round the back of the palace.

The gaol was linked up to the barracks, where the Royal Guards were based.

And where Herimyre was based.

She instructed him that once he'd killed Herimyre, stabbed him with the Webbing Blade, she would be free to use her magic at will—to destroy the rest of the guards.

He was to signal to her with a *ca-kaw* call, just like the ones those cursed crows had made as they'd descended upon them.

Lou knew he wouldn't forget the signal in a hurry.

Lou could hear his heart throbbing in his ears, and his legs barely obeying his brain's commands for him to keep moving.

Hildie had told him that one of the basics of stealth was simply to keep moving. And he tried to take that lesson to heart.

The scent of roses here, the freshly cut grass, was almost overwhelming. When he breathed in he tasted the moist dew layering onto his tongue. Up ahead he could see a torch burning steadily above what he supposed to be the main entrance to the palace.

Now, in the dead of night, there were no other torches about the palace.

He guessed that the king liked darkness to sleep.

Hildie reached back and took his hand with her gloved one. He gazed at that leather glove of hers, sheening a little in the torchlight coming from the entrance of the palace.

She had told him in no uncertain terms that he could destroy her if he wished, just from touching his skin to hers. But Lou still hadn't quite decided just what he might do with that knowledge.

If he'd ever do anything at all.

He listened to the grass beneath their gentle tread, as it brushed against their boots.

Hildie squeezed his hand tighter and led him on, up to the wall of the palace. And they sidled their way along the wall, keeping themselves flush to the stone.

And then, from up ahead, Lou heard gentle, tuneless whistling.

Hildie pressed her hand to his chest, pushing him back against the wall.

Lou's spine hit the stone hard, but he suppressed the pain, sinking his teeth into his lower lip. And the two of them stood there, motionless, Lou scoping out the area ahead, trying to work out just where the whistling was coming from.

He listened to Hildie's breathing, felt her warm breath blow against his cheeks. And he felt that soft glow within himself again, spreading out from her fingertips, from where she touched his chest.

She'd also told him, back at her house, that as he got more in touch with his ice magic that he would find it harder and harder to touch her too. Soon enough they would hardly be able to stand in the room together.

If Lou chose to get in touch with his ice magic, that was.

Lou watched as a guard rounded the corner. He held his spear in his hand, leaning up against his shoulder, its blade pointing up to the night sky. As the guard trudged along, he pursed his lips and whistled that incessant, tuneless tune. His lazy bootfalls acting as a kind of percussion to his shredded melody.

And then he stopped with his back to them.

Lou was on the cusp of asking Hildie just what they were going to do next, when she darted away from him, padding along quickly, and then, just as the guard turned round at the sound of the footsteps, she held up her hand and Lou watched on as she flamed his throat.

The guard dropped down, his mouth jabbering away but no sound coming out. He made a *thud* as he landed on the cobblestones. And Lou smelled the burned flesh carrying on the breeze.

Hildie glanced back at Lou and waved him onwards.

As Lou passed by the dead man, staring up into the moonless night sky, lips slightly parted, Lou thought of something else that Hildie had said to him before they'd left her house.

She'd told him that, if it hadn't been for Lou, then she could've got through the palace gardens invisible. And so Lou couldn't help thinking he was somewhat responsible for the man's death. It was an effort to keep him from being discovered.

He had no idea *how* to make himself invisible. But, then again, he guessed that in turn he was keeping *her* safe, since she wouldn't be able to face Herimyre herself.

She needed him to stick the Blade in.

They snuck their way onwards without encountering any further resistance. And only when they reached the barracks, its darkened, blocky shape in the near total darkness, did Lou begin to feel something approaching completely paralysing fear.

He . . . he couldn't do this.

He could *kill* this man.

Could he?

25

THE BARRACKS

HILDIE GLANCED to him, her eyes sparkling with what Lou swore to be flames. "Go on," she said, nodding to the ledge there, to the strong creeping vines that ran up the trellis, and up the side of the barracks wall.

He looked to the trellis, to those cross-hatched wooden supports, and he wondered if they'd really take his weight. She had told him to simply keep climbing up. To get up as quickly as he could.

And not to look down.

Now, though, looking at it, Lou was almost certain that he couldn't climb up. He felt those familiar nerves creeping back in, playing on his mind.

He saw a thousand horrifying scenarios play out in his mind: him slipping from the trellis, flying backwards through the air then landing on his back. He could almost hear the *snap* of the wood giving way beneath his boots.

And then he thought of Syre, and everything else disappeared from his mind.

He stepped up onto the trellis, concentrating on his footholds, keeping himself steady, not allowing himself to look down, just like Hildie said.

When he had got up past four storeys, he felt the wind blowing in, rustling his cloak against him. He felt the rough material brush his skin, the wood biting into his hands, but he kept going.

On and up.

Till he reached the ledge.

His stomach dipped away from him as he reached out for the window. He got his fingers round its frame, and then tested his weight. The opening was made of stone, of course. And deep down he knew that it would hold him. But he refused to admit to himself that he was afraid.

He pushed off from the trellis, taking a little leap into the air, and he gripped hold of the stone window ledge.

For a heart-stopping second, he felt his legs swaying freely below him, waving in the air, and then he caught the side of the building, found a foothold there, and he lugged himself inside, through the window, landing on the hard stone floor.

Lou looked about him.

He was in a corridor, the corridor on the top floor of the barracks. He glanced up and down it, saw no one was there, and then clambered back up to his feet.

He stared out through the window, back down to the ground, out across the palace gardens. He looked to where Hildie had been, where he'd imagined to see her, standing and watching on, but now she'd gone. Slipped off somewhere into the shadows. Now he was on his own.

He had to kill Herimyre so that she might spring his people from the barracks.

He snuck his way along the stone corridor, along to the door at the end of it, the one behind which Herimyre slept. Again he felt that slight tremor of fear pass through him.

Or was it from the frostiness of the Webbing Blade?

As he approached the door, drew closer and closer, he reached for the handle of the dagger, ready to slip it from its sheath. Although he'd got to the point where he could tolerate holding the dagger for several minutes without it becoming too much to bear, he didn't want to hold it in his hand until it was the right time.

He stole closer still, so that he was by the doorknob now, and, sucking in a lungful of air, he reached out for the doorknob, took it in his fist.

As he turned it, felt the mechanism click, imagined its whirring in his mind, its snicking into place, he clasped his eyes shut, like a child trying to escape from a living nightmare.

This was his life now.

If he wanted to save his people then he had to be a hero.

He had to kill the man that had imprisoned them.

With a smart, final *click*, the mechanism slid back and his own weight seemed to push the door back into the room.

He was hit by overpowering darkness, gloom all around.

He reached for the Webbing Blade, its handle, and he slid it gently from its sheath.

Ready to do his duty.

That first flushing chill grabbed him like a bath in an iced-over river.

Once, when he'd been younger, about ten or eleven summers old, he'd gone off with a bunch of other boys from the village, down to a creek in the woods in the heart of winter. And he remembered how they'd dared one another to walk over the iced-over river, to take ever so gentle steps over to the other side.

Lou recalled how he'd watched on, seen each of his companions get across safely, no more than a couple of thin cracks appearing in the ice beneath their boots, and then, feeling that throb of confidence, he'd done the same. And he'd been so sure that he'd made it across.

And then, of course, he'd heard that gut-wrenching *crack*, and the whole world had broken up beneath his feet.

And he'd plunged into that icy water.

He remembered that he'd spent the rest of the winter tucked up in bed, taking all kinds of his mother's remedies, nothing seeming to have any effect. He had shuddered as he'd laid beneath those blankets, never really thawing till he'd felt the warmth of the spring sun shining in through his window.

And Hildie told him that he had ice magic in his veins.

Ice magic hadn't done anything for him back then. He had almost died from the cold

... or was it really that simple?

Perhaps the ice magic *had* saved him. He remembered clearly the grim faces of the adults that'd come to see him tucked up in bed.

Those grim faces reserved for the very particular trauma of a dying child.

As Lou stepped further into the room, his heart beat so hard that he was sure that the sleeping Captain of the Royal Guards would certainly hear it.

But, from within the room, all Lou heard was gentle snoring.

Nothing else.

Just that heavy breathing.

For a second he found himself rendered static, he simply couldn't put one foot in front of the other any longer. He stood there, in the darkness, feeling the gloom tremor over his skin.

What he was about to do went against everything he'd been taught. All the things he'd learned at school, about fair fighting, and those hundreds of stories he'd heard about the ignobility of stabbing someone in the back.

Wasn't that just what he was doing now?

. . . But wasn't there a good reason for it?

These men had taken his people unjustly, they had got in the way of his people's refuge, and now this was what it had come down to.

He stepped closer and closer.

He caught a strong whiff of Herimyre's musky scent in the air, and that heavy breathing still came thick and hard.

He could smell the trace of tobacco in the air too, almost stifling. And he could taste it at the back of his mouth, and some memory of having tried to smoke a pipe when he'd been young and impressionable struck him.

He gripped the Webbing Blade hard in his fist, feeling its icy-burn pound through his bloodstream, becoming part of him, just an extension of his hand.

He had to do this.

And he had to do this *now*.

He took the final few steps, over to the bedside, and staring into the gloom, his eyes just about getting used to the almost absent light, he picked out the shape nestled in the sheets below him.

He gripped the Webbing Blade tight and then brought it down, right into place he guessed to be Herimyre's chest.

Lou felt the Webbing Blade plunge into the chest, far too easily to be dealing with the thickness of ribs, or even the squidgy resistance of internal organs.

But he tried not to think about it.

Only when he felt the warm spurt of blood on his skin did he think to retreat, to pull the blade back out of Herimyre's skin.

He watched the man, there in the bed, only able to make out his basic shape. And yet he was sure he could see him there, his head tilted to one side, staring right at him.

Yes, he was certain.

Herimyre was looking at him, eyeballing him, his lips shuddering with the chill from the Webbing Blade, and his whole body rigid with the ice magic purging his body.

They stared at one another for a long time.

Lou was sure that Herimyre would break out of this rigid pose any second and scream out for help, that there would be the sound of dozens of boots as half the barracks rushed up the stairs, came to slaughter Lou where he stood.

To take the Webbing Blade from him.

But no one came.

And, seconds later, with a final drawing of breath, Herimyre's chest slumped down for the final time.

He was dead.

Lou wasn't sure how to explain the feeling, how he knew for certain that Herimyre was dead. He supposed that the air had grown heavier, and a chill had added a snap to it.

And then he remembered the Webbing Blade, which he still held in his fist.

He looked to it, saw the bloody smear there in the half-light, and, not really thinking, wiped it clean with the bed sheet. Then he replaced it in its sheath and padded back out into the corridor. And he called out through the window, down to Hildie, wherever she might be waiting in the palace gardens.

"*Ca-Kaw!*"

Lou listened to his call reverberate about the palace walls, come back at him two or three times. And then he stared out into the gloom of the gardens, hoping to catch sight of Hildie, for her to reassure him in some way. Then, just as he scanned the garden for a fifth time, searching desperately for her, a terrible feeling struck him.

What if she'd simply disappeared from the place?

Gone off back to her house, escaped from here?

What was there in this for her to stay?

And then he remembered what she'd said about raising an army. But was that what she'd really wanted, or just a sleight of hand?

All those doubts vanished from his mind, though, in a second, as he felt the rising heat against his cheeks, that stink of ash taking to the air.

And he knew that it couldn't be anything else but fire magic.

The feeling was strange when it struck him. A kind of nausea in the pit of his stomach, which rose through him, tickled his oesophagus. He tasted bile at the back of his throat, but he swallowed it back down.

He felt sweat dampen his face, but he wiped it away with the sleeve of his cloak. For some reason his hand felt drawn to the handle of the Webbing Blade, and he reached for it, touched it with his bare fingertips.

And it reassured him.

Almost eliminated that nauseous feeling right away.

All of a sudden he felt better.

Sturdier.

More confident.

And then the screams began.

26

PALACE GAOL

BEFORE HE KNEW just where he was headed, his feet carried him. They carried him along the corridor, that slap of stone beneath his boots. And he leaped at the trellis which hung at the side of the barracks, working his hands down it as he went, his stomach falling away from him several times as his brain was certain he was about to tumble down to the hard ground.

When he made it back down to the soft palace lawn, he saw the guards crawling along the ramparts, their bodies silhouettes against the now-rising sun.

One of them shot a crossbow.

Lou dived to his side, crunching into a bush beside him. He felt the branches stick into his skin, jab him in the ribs. But he lay there, hidden inside it. He breathed in the smell of the leaves, and could still taste that ash in the air.

He knew that Hildie was close by, that she was working her fire magic.

A bolt whistled through the air, and clattered into the stone wall just behind Lou's head. He ducked after he heard it clatter.

If these were what his reflexes were like then he might be better served staying here, staying hidden. But he knew he had to move out of this place. He had to get to the others.

Find them.

He peered out through the leaves of the bush, up to the ramparts. He saw the guards speaking among themselves, both stooped over, trying to see him there in the dawning morning light.

They pointed towards where Lou was, but he was almost certain that he was well hidden. Sure they could pepper him with crossbow bolts, but he was pretty sure they wouldn't be able to target anything in particular.

He felt his chest heave against his tunic, his throat stick several times with his breaths. He could feel his body locking up, his muscles knotting as he got caught in a panic. He was trapped here.

If only they would fire off some more of the those bolts, then—

As Lou looked out from behind those leaves, he watched as a ball of fire seared through the air and consumed the two guards. He felt the heat on his cheeks, rip right through him, even though he was some way away. He reached down for the Webbing Blade. Just touched his fingers to its handle. He felt that reassuring icy spark sizzle through his fingertips, worm its way through his veins, and slow his heartbeat.

When the fire cleared, Lou saw that nothing was left. Just the charred remains of the guards, which crumbled then blew away on the morning wind. And he tilted his head to look up at the ramparts, to where he saw Hildie emerging.

She was staring into the darkness, looking all over the palace gardens for him.

Lou's first urge was to get to his feet, for him to wave to her, to show her just where he was. But doubt sprouted inside him, and he stayed still.

What was the matter? Was it that he didn't trust her? Of course he didn't trust her. She had ruined his home, murdered his parents, driven him to murder.

If he wished, he could just sit tight here, pretend like he was invisible.

See just what she had planned.

And then, through the rising morning mist, now fogging its way up the palace walls—the same walls that would keep the cursed animals back—she called out to him. "Lou! Lou! I've found them!"

Lou breathed in deep several times, felt his heart lodge in his throat, got that unpleasant fluttering sensation on the back of his tongue, and then, reluctantly, got to his feet and showed her just where he was hidden.

Lou padded his way up the winding stone stairs, breathing in the coolness of the stone—the stone that would soon take on a completely different smell when the sun rose. He kept his finger-tips on the handle of the Webbing Blade, not wanting to ever let go of it.

The dagger reassured him, it told him that everything was okay, and that he would get through this.

And it told him something else.

It told him that he wasn't simply another working hand, that he had only been born for a life out in the fields, it told him that he could be so much more.

If he wanted.

He could be an *ice mage*.

Hildie grabbed hold of his other hand, the one that didn't grasp the handle of the Webbing Blade, and led him after her, skirting the ramparts, barrelling their way onwards, back towards the barracks, to what Lou soon saw was the palace gaol.

He took in the place.

Whereas the rest of the city—the rest of Ilsnare—had all those distinctive crystal roofs, the *gaol* was carved out of the same stone that they used for the walls. That same pit-black colour from the Sable Mountains, the shade that Lou would never ever forget after those hobblesmen had come to Endmere with those paintings of theirs.

Up ahead was the entrance, or what had been the entrance: a wooden door reinforced with iron. Now, though, all that was left of it was the iron melted into the stone floor. The wooden was only ashes. Lou glanced to it briefly as Hildie tugged him onwards, into the gaol.

He felt that warmth permeate her leather gloves, brush against his palm. And it gave him an unpleasant tickling sensation. A sensation he could only tolerate by gripping the handle of the Webbing Blade tight with his other hand.

Inside the gaol, the air was thick and humid, and Lou could hear water dripping somewhere off in the distance.

Hildie tightened her hold on his hand, and Lou breathed in the damp of the place, that mixture of stone and musk and excrement. He could hear the gentle bustle of people nearby: that scuffing of feet, coughing and grumbling that signals a bunch of people are crowded close by.

He remembered when he'd been a child, when some hobblesmen had brought false fires to their town, and how they'd lit them up in the evening, let them whizz into the night sky where they exploded in bursts of colour: neon pinks, iridescent greens, and deep mauves.

That smell, the tangy stench of the false fires, came back to him too now.

And it reminded him of just how Hildie's fire magic smelled.

Hildie dragged him down several sets of spiralling stairs.

The air got thicker still.

The odours almost intolerable.

Lou felt his stomach churn, and felt the warm rise of bile inside. He swallowed long and hard, and concentrated on the Webbing Blade which he kept his fingers fixed to.

Soon enough they reached the base of the spiral stairs. The floor beneath their feet flattened out, and Lou spun round, trying to force his eyes to adapt to the gloom coming in at him from all sides, trying to get a grip on the faint light which came from a flickering torch down off deeper in the dungeon.

Hildie dragged him on, and then he saw the cell. All spread out before them. The cold, iron bars, and those desolate, miserable faces crammed right between them.

This was it.

They'd found them.

Lou quickly spun through the faces, casting each one of them off as he went. He saw the sparkle in their eyes, as they took in Lou, as they recognised him as not being a Royal Guard, but being that working hand, now rookie skuller, they'd often seen about town. That quiet young man who'd never really made much of an impression on anything.

He was making an impression now.

He glanced back to Hildie.

She had released his hand and was already ordering the prisoners back from the bars, telling them to get as far back as they could.

Lou stared over the faces of the prisoners, all trapped inside that cell, and he tried to pick out Syre, but he had no luck. He couldn't see her anywhere. And then, between a couple of bulky men, men who'd also been working hands back in Endmere—he recognised their faces but couldn't have summoned their names for the life of him—he saw her.

Syre.

And she saw him.

Her eyes lit up, and she made to take a step forward. Only Hildie's ordering her back again checked her steps towards him.

Hildie held her hand to the locking mechanism, and Lou watched side on as her palm glowed and then smoke rose from it as she pressed it to the lock. He watched the metal grow white-hot and then seem to fold in on itself. And then the mechanism simply dropped off the iron bars, and clanked onto the ground, at Hildie's feet.

She turned to him, gave him a brief smile, then kicked the door to the cell open.

The hinges howled and then the gate jerked back into the stone wall. The prisoners stayed back where they were, in the darkness, reminding Lou a little of when he'd worked with cows back on Old Man Junth's farm, and how they'd hang back when he went to get them from their barn in the morning, staying away from the daylight.

And then they slouched forwards, making their way across the stone floor, and he picked out Syre among them, and before he knew what was happening, she rushed into his arms, threw her arms around him. They embraced there, while the rest of the prisoners poured out around him, some of them pausing briefly to give him a slap on the shoulder.

When Lou prised Syre away from his chest, looked about the cell, he realised that it had emptied quickly, and then, right there, at the back, he saw that book lying there. What had been their ma's book.

A Practical Understanding of Dark Magic.

He stared at it a long time as he held tight onto Syre's hand, and he'd half-turned away from it, ready for them to beat their retreat from the gaol with the rest of their people, when Syre tugged on his fingers, and then let go of his hand.

She danced across the cell and stooped for the book. She took it back in her arms and then clutched it to her chest, grinning as she skipped back up to him. "We can go now," she said, still grinning.

The prisoners crammed their way up the spiral staircases. As Lou tugged Syre after him, he felt her feet tripping several times. But he caught her each time before she fell right over. He guessed that he still had most of his muscles built up from bringing in the yield. At least he had no trouble in lugging a ten-year-old girl after him.

They reached the level of the palace walls again, and Lou savoured the fresh air wafting in through the gaol, from the outside. He thought he could smell the morning mist too, laying down its curses, sending all untethered animals from all around into some kind of fury.

Into their *cursed* state.

Lou pushed it out of his mind, told himself that they now had a fire mage among them, that she could simply destroy all resistance without issue.

And Lou had killed Herimyre.

So the cursed animals were all he they had to contend with. And he reminded himself that now he had the Webbing Blade.

They rushed on along the walls till they heard someone call out from above. Just like the others, Lou came to a halt and glanced back over his shoulder.

He took in the man, standing up at the top of the barracks. Staring down at them, his arms spread shoulder-width apart on the ledge, looking out.

Although he was a long way away, Lou was certain he could see his eyes bulging from their sockets, the veins sticking up on his face, the pure, unchecked rage there.

And he was bellowing at them.

Lou had no need to look to Hildie to realise just who this was.

Herimyre, Captain of the Royal Guards.

27

DAWN'S SIREN

LOU FELT his mind ebbing away inside his skull. He felt his thoughts rush and draw. He tried to get a grip on his thoughts again, but they kept spinning away from him, slipping from his grasp.

Herimyre was dead.

He'd slipped the Webbing Blade into his chest himself.

While Herimyre had been sleeping.

He was gone.

He must, then, be mistaken in his assumption, that this wasn't the Captain of the Royal Guards at all, and this time he did look to Hildie. Her eyes met his and then he knew for sure.

He had killed someone else.

Before Lou had the chance to get things straight, Hildie glared at him then said, "Get them out, get your people out!"

Lou looked over the prisoners, all of them gawping at Herimyre, standing up there on that open corridor that led to the bedroom of the man he'd killed, and then Lou barked the order to them.

They all followed him, snapping out of their daze.

Hildie stood firm as the prisoners rushed about her, and Lou, the last of them to escape, looked to her. She met his eye briefly, and then reached out and took his hand in hers. She gave it a light squeeze, gave him the hint of a smile, and then said, "Meet me out at the forest. If I'm not there by sundown then do what you can."

Do what you can?

Lou thought that to himself several times over.

If they got out there, out on the plains, and the sunset caught them, then they'd be mincemeat. The cursed animals would see them off. Even if he did have the Webbing Blade.

He knew that at most he might be able to see off a cursed sheep, but a pack of bears or wolves, that would be a different matter.

Without Hildie those cursed crows would've pecked him to death.

But he put his concerns to one side for the time being and he sprinted after the others, quickly retreating from the palace, heading out through the busted gate, and into Ilsnare.

The gate alongside the palace, which led out onto the plains, was unguarded.

Lou knew that the toil at the palace must've taken its toll with the watchmen, and now he knew that he hadn't killed Herimyre he knew that the remaining Royal Guards, the ones that Hildie hadn't killed in their beds, had been roused from whatever post they were manning and ordered back to the palace.

In the early morning light, the mist rising off the land, and the threat of cursed animal attacks slipping away to nothing for another twelve hours, Lou ran his way to the head of the group and he led them on, through the long grasses, keeping a fair distance from the walls of Ilsnare so that any remaining guards on the walls wouldn't see them.

About twenty minutes later he heard a roar of what he imagined to be a stiff breeze kicking up on their heels.

When Lou looked round, though, he saw an almighty jet of fire bursting into the sky, almost eclipsing the sun.

All of them stopped to marvel at the sight. And Lou could feel the heat of it against his cheek, just watching on. That ash carried on the boiling wind, and then, as the flames descended and the sunlight regained its dominion, he led his people onwards, across the plains.

Once they'd got a safe distance away, he slowed the pace, allowed his people to have their rest. And they trudged their way around the city, and into the midday sun without pause.

A little while later and they made the hill with the forest towards its back. And Lou knew just why Hildie had picked it as being their rendezvous point. That she had every intention of using the forest as cover for their getaway.

They would simply disappear from anybody watching on from the ramparts of Ilsnare.

He allowed the people to stop, for them to keel over and rest. He instructed them to get sleep while they could, that soon enough they would be running away once again.

Once Hildie came back to them.

If she came back to them.

The sun was on its way down, and Lou was thinking about doing just what Hildie had suggested, about them 'doing the best they could' as he saw that familiar, cloaked figure appearing across the plains.

That stooped posture of the hobblesman.

He watched as the sun set over her shoulder, as she grew closer still, became more of a silhouette. This time, though, as she trod her way up the hillside path, he could penetrate that shadow with his gaze, he could see her face there. She drew closer and he felt that warmth rising in his blood once more, coming back to him.

And before he knew it, she stood before him.

Lou fumbled for the words. "Did you find Rut and Sully? They weren't with the others. They're not with us now." He paused, realising that Hildie had no idea who they were. "Skullers, they're skullers too," he added hastily.

She smiled faintly. "Don't you think I know who they are? Who do you think set that old lady's hair on fire—got you sprung from that gaoler's cart?"

Another piece of the puzzle slipped into place for Lou, although he supposed that he'd already expected just as much.

"Us mages, we've got to stick together." She breathed a sigh. "I couldn't have saved all three of you, that would've been too much for me to take on. Then one of you really might've chopped my head off," she said, with a smile again, but Lou saw, at the backs of those emerald eyes, that she wasn't joking. "Mortals are unpredictable."

Lou knew he would have to save Rut and Sully.

That he would have to go back and get them.

But surely his priority was to get the rest of his people safe. Then he could go off gallivanting with his heroics again.

He glanced back to Ilsnare, to the light from the setting sun sending all those rooftops aflame, and then he looked to Hildie. "What was that burst of fire, that we saw back at the plains? It was incredible."

She kept up that light, slightly absent-minded smile. "That's a spell known as Dawn's Siren, only works at dawn, like the name suggests. It harnesses the power of the sun. One of the most powerful spells in a fire mage's arsenal."

She stared at her feet. "My father taught it to me. But it tires me." She looked up, to the trees, to the forest behind them. "We'd better get moving soon. Those trees will give us good cover, and I should be able to take care of most cursed animals that come for us in there. No real chance of them getting us surrounded. Not with all the foliage there."

She glanced back at him, catching his eye. "We won't see them coming, though, that's the only problem."

Lou reached for the Webbing Blade, felt that now-reassuring chill pass through his fingertips. And then he stared into Hildie's eyes for a long time before speaking again. Before reeling off what was really on his mind. "Back at the palace," he said. "Who did I kill if not Herimyre?"

Her smile completely slipped from her lips now, and she averted his gaze. She looked back over at Ilsnare, and then he saw the left sleeve of her cloak was a black colour, damp with some liquid.

A moment later and he twigged that it was blood.

That her hand was bleeding.

He looked at her face in profile again.

She smile lightly in profile, still gazing back off in the direction of The Crystal City—its rooftops now reaching the zenith of their glow in the sunset, all grapefruit pinks and sheening gold. "Herimyre. You wouldn't think he's mortal, but he is. He knows how to get close to us, how to see through all but our strongest spells, how to deal us harm." She rolled back her sleeve, without looking back at Lou, and exposed her hand.

It'd been clear sliced off. And he saw that the stump was burned up, scorched flesh.

She rolled her sleeve back down to cover the stump, met his eye briefly. "Good thing about being a fire mage is that I've got more than a few medical charms tucked away. Trouble is that most of them are for patching things up, rather than performing any lasting repair." She met his eye again. "If you manage to get a hold on your powers, though, you might be able to help me out. Ice magic's the only thing that can put me right now."

Lou swore to himself that he really could do it, that he would work hard if only to repay Hildie for helping him rescue his people, whatever her agenda.

In his gut now he knew it, on instinct, that what she said was true—that as mages they had to stick together.

And he was determined to keep learning, to keep finding out more about his powers. Whether or not he got himself interested in her war—this coming *magical* war—was another matter, though.

His priority now was to get these people safe, to get them as far away from The Crystal City as possible.

He looked back to Hildie again. "You didn't answer my question, about who I killed, back at the barracks."

He watched the rise and fall of her chest against her cloak, as her red hair rose with her respiration, catching a little of the setting sun in its strands. "The king," she said. "You killed the king."

Lou felt his knees buckle, and all the strength leave his body momentarily. His vision went blurry and blood pounded up to his temples. He knew he had killed.

But . . . the *king?*

The King of Shellacnass?

That was almost beyond comprehension for him. Impossible to understand.

And before fully got a grip on it, he felt that warmth of Hildie's fingertips against his upper arm, her leading him away from The Crystal City, away from everything they'd done there, and towards the forest, to their future.

Their redemption.

But as she led him away, into the gloom of the forest gathering round them, he couldn't help but sneak a final glance back to Ilsnare, to look The Crystal City over one last time.

And just at that moment, he saw the sun dipping down behind the horizon for the final time, the glow dissipating from the crystal rooftops, and those rooftops just becoming glass—taking on that colourless, grey tone—beginning to take on the shade of the mist as it rolled over the whole city.

Bringing its twice-daily curse down once again.

And then Lou turned round, and faced up to the forest

approaching them. He reached down for the Webbing Blade, felt its chilly tickle against his fingertips. And he found comfort there. A tickling comfort purging through his blood. That *ice* magic keeping him safe.

Keeping all of them safe.

28

A CURSE IS CAST

M A'REYGAR listened in hard for any sound.

But there was only the stirring of the wind in the distant trees, the trees back on the plains. He would be back there soon, he would be safe.

And he was determined that he would bring his wife back with him. It wasn't right that his daughter should grow without a mother. And that sense of justice drove him on.

He felt the stone ledge of the king's chamber beneath his fingers. That delightful chill ran through him, the same chill he got whenever he touched his wife, whenever their skin touched.

He had to keep her weak, of course, weak enough that they could still touch. But that channel of ice magic in her blood, that was enough to keep that thrill alive for him. And soon they'd be reunited.

Herimyre would be foolish to crop up now, to try and stop him.

It might mean death for both of them.

And, in the half-light, he made out the king, sleeping in his four-poster bed, those flimsy, transparent curtains collected round him, giving him privacy.

Ma'reygar stalked closer, feeling the Webbing Blade in its sheath, at his side. He would leave it till the right time. His hands were still shaking from his killing the guard on the ramparts. He should've held off till now, had more patience. But the thrill, the temptation of slicing the man's throat with the Webbing Blade, had just proved too strong.

He stood over the king's bed now. He could hear the gentle breathing of the man, see his form in the half-light, and he breathed in the light musk of the place, that thick . . . *kingly* scent.

This man who wasn't fit to be a king at all.

And then, from the corner of the chamber, he heard the voice he'd feared all along. The light timbre that made his nerves tremble, sent a shudder right up his spine.

He swung round to see there, standing in the corner of the room, was Herimyre himself.

Unmistakable even in the darkness.

Those broad shoulders, the almost impossibly square chin, and the broad sword in the sheath down at his side.

Tysron.

That was the name of the sword. Some mage, in the Sable Mountains, had forged it for Herimyre. It resisted magic.

Merely beat it away as a monk thrashes a petulant child in the classroom.

"I thought you'd come, *mage*," Herimyre said, out of the darkness.

Ma'reygar stood firm, afraid to say anything. His fingertips just lingering over the Webbing Blade, over its handle, already feeling that crispy chill, and feeling it fighting back against his fire magic, even through the bandage he'd bundled round the handle so he might be able to wield it a little while.

Ma'reygar's throat felt dry, and his mouth as if it'd been bathed in some pestilent stench, but he managed to force himself into thinking, into telling himself why he was here.

He was here for his wife.

And he would save her.

He swore it.

"You know why I'm here," Ma'reygar said.

Herimyre stepped out of the corner of the king's quarters. He paused after a few steps, and reached for the handle of his sword.

For the handle of Tysron.

But he stopped short of drawing it from its sheath.

Ma'reygar felt Herimyre's eyes on his, felt their weight on his skin. And he couldn't help but think of Tysron, that sword of his.

Ma'reygar could hear Herimyre's breathing, almost feel its moist warmth pooling against his cheeks, and it turned his stomach, seemed to make those chilly waves coming off the Webbing Blade come all the stronger.

But he stood firm and proud.

He would not be made to flee.

He would be the one to decide when, or whether, he fled.

"You've come for your wife," Herimyre said, his voice measured, steady.

Ma'reygar felt his heart throb in his chest. He bit his tongue and tasted blood, not wanting to cry out, to burst out into a rage that might see him killed, his daughter orphaned, left out there where he'd left her wrapped up in those silk blankets hidden in the spliced tangle of tree roots.

The king breathed more heavily from his bed, and Ma'reygar sensed that he had woken up, that he was looking between the two shadowy figures who were inside his quarters, watching this face off take place.

And then, just to confirm it, the king spoke.

"Your wife is dead. We *executed* the wench."

The king's voice was sharp, without pity. Filled with gloating and pride. As if this was a wonderful act that he'd perpetrated. The very height of statesmanship, of servitude.

Ma'reygar felt himself caught in a swirl. The chill of the Webbing Blade clawing at his thigh, as if freezing his blood vessels to his skin.

He wasn't sure who moved first, him or Herimyre, but before he knew it, Herimyre had drawn Tysron and he was swinging away, bringing it swishing through the air, down in a spiral, intending to throttle Ma'reygar.

Ma'reygar dodged out the way, barrelled over onto his side and rolled his way over the window. He listened to the steady heft of Herimyre's bootfalls, coming after him, but Ma'reygar was too quick. He'd already made it to the windowsill. Already felt the chill beneath his fingertips as he took hold of the stone, the smoothness against his palms, and he tossed himself over, back out onto the ramparts.

Ma'reygar beat his retreat along the ramparts, feeling Herimyre's eyes on his back as he went. Ma'reygar had no need to even try to use his magic, he knew it would be in vain. All that he'd ever heard about Tysron he now knew, just from his gut, to be correct.

That . . . that *thing* could melt all his powers away, render him weak as a lamb.

As Ma'reygar stood on the hill, having escaped from Ilsnare, he looked back across The Crystal City, and he saw the dawn rising on the horizon.

He felt the rage knot more and more inside him, grow into an all-out tangle.

And he knew the only way that he would ever dispel that rage was to seek his revenge.

No.

Have his revenge.

But it would take time. And planning. To bring these mortals to their knees—*all* these mortals—to bring them down to the place where they deserved.

And then, over his shoulder, from within the forest he heard the gentle sob of his daughter—of Hilda, his Hildie.

He tilted his head back to listen to her.

Funny the fears of a child.

And then it struck him.

How he might leave these mortals with something hanging over them while he plotted his true revenge.

He had heard about the curses, about how the mingling of fire and ice magic could yield terrible things. Truly awful circumstances that could come to bear over a land for years and years, for several decades. And that, to Ma'reygar, seemed like a just time for them to mull over just what they'd done to him.

Taking away his sweet, *innocent* wife.

He closed his eyes and reached for the Webbing Blade.

That icy chill ran through those bandages and he felt its burning cool against his palm. But he clung onto the handle, determined that he would go through with this, that he would cast the curse that would ensure these mortals would fear him forever more.

No, more than that.

He would give them a *real* reason for them to fear magic.

He clasped the Webbing Blade in his fist and his staff in the other and he spoke to the deepest parts of himself, scraped the very pits of his soul, accessed that area which he knew was the very worst of himself.

The suppressed rage of all those years.

All those frustrations with the mortal realm.

And then, with the sun rising in the corner of his eye, he let loose a mighty scream, which echoed over the plains, bounced back off those walls of Ilsnare and, he fancied, sent those crystal rooftops trembling.

All the powers within him roared out in a fitful burst of flame and sodden ash.

But there was something else now.

As he gently opened his eyes he saw the blood pouring down his hands from where he clasped hold of the Webbing Blade. And he saw it dripping frozen blood too. Those frozen crystals which spiralled through the air and then clinked down at his feet in the dewy long grass.

And that firestorm that rose above him, those swirls and icy rages all congealed and floated off in the direction of the sun, and over to Ilsnare to linger there forever more.

And, as he watched the cloud of fire sweep over The Crystal City, he knew that what he'd done had appeased his rage.

For now.

Hildie's cries grew louder, more difficult to ignore.

Ma'reygar turned and looked back into the darkness of the forest, penetrated its gloom with his gaze. Soon it would be a new day, and the dawn would bring a fresh curse with it for Ilsnare and its people. The mortals would have to learn to live with themselves, swearing against the day they'd wronged him.

And then he would return, and he would really give them something to scream about.

Because, for too long, magic had lived as a second-class citizen, permitting all these small violations against its ethereal soul.

And now, Ma'reygar was determined that magic would have its sweet vengeance.

Ma'reygar stepped through the long grass, feeling it dampen his trousers. He breathed in the freshness of the plains, the morning dew. He could taste its moisture in his mouth, and, a little way away, he was sure he could hear a far away scream carrying on the morning breeze.

Or perhaps it was just his mind getting carried away, as it had a habit of doing.

As he crunched over branches lying on the floor of the forest, he stooped down over Hildie, saw her there, mewling away in her silk bundle. He lifted her up in his arms and looked at that peachy face of hers, that bright red hair that matched his own.

And he thought about how she was his daughter.

He would teach her that fire flowed from her fingertips, and he would teach her that she no longer had to suffer at the hands of the oppression her mother had suffered. She would be well and truly free.

Forever.

He would see to that.

But now was a time for reconciliation, a time for him to raise his daughter in peace. Let the mortals fight against his curse for a time, let them suffer as he'd suffered, never fully knowing whether or not he would return, the most powerful mages in the land at his side . . . and then one day he *would*. Perhaps even with Hildie alongside him.

He would see to it that she became a fearsome fire mage.

And as he walked on, entering the forest, feeling the warmth of the morning sun settle onto the leaves of the trees, gently heat up the canopy, and send those bright, fresh scents of flowers and grass up his nostrils, he saw a brighter world.

A world in which he would be king.

AUTHOR'S NOTE

Thank you for taking the time to read one of my books. If you would like to hear about my latest releases you can sign up for my newsletter here: www.raymondsflex.com

Thanks for reading!

Raymond S Flex

The Webbing Blade
The First Crystal Kingdom Novel